WEIRD
LITTLE
ROBOTS

WEIRD
LITTLE
ROBOTS

Carolyn Crimi

illustrated by

Corinna Luyken

CK PRESS

Text copyright © 2019 by Carolyn Crimi
Illustrations copyright © 2019 by Corinna Luyken
Hand-lettering on page 234 by Quinn Pappidas

First edition 2019

Library of Congress Catalog Card Number 2019939115
ISBN 978-0-7636-9493-7

19 20 21 22 23 24 LSC 10 9 8 7 6 5 4 3 2 1

Printed in Crawfordsville, IN, U.S.A.

This book was typeset in Mendoza.
The illustrations were done in ink, pencil, and gouache.

Candlewick Press
99 Dover Street
Somerville, Massachusetts 02144

visit us at www.candlewick.com

MIX
Paper from
responsible sources
FSC® C132124

For my amazing writers' group—
Sarah Aronson, Brenda Ferber,
Jenny Meyerhoff, and Laura Ruby
C. C.

For Cora and Quinn
C. L.

The cool September breeze blew down from the north. It drifted through Darkling Forest, causing the animals there to burrow deeper into their underground homes. It picked up leaves and gum wrappers as it whooshed across Skillington Avenue. It swept past the Boilses' house, the Hinkles' house, and the Gilmores' house until it settled over the very last house on the corner, number 1959.

You might not pay too much attention to this old Victorian at first. Its front yard was ordinary enough. The ordinary porch swing creaked in the wind. Two ordinary pots of yellow mums welcomed guests.

But if you walked around to the *back*yard, you would see a shed with a sagging roof and cracked windows. An interesting shed. A sign written in crayon was taped to its green door:

DON'T COME IN — I'M CREATING.

And if you looked through the window of the shed on that September afternoon, you'd see an eleven-year-old girl named Penny Rose Mooney sitting at a rickety card table with more than a dozen items strewn across it.

There were the usual helpful things, like the hammer that was no bigger than a pencil, the wing nuts, the screwdriver, and the cigar box filled with triple-A batteries. Penny Rose especially loved the yellow metal tape measure that zipped back into its case with the touch of a button.

But most fascinating of all were the little robots that Penny Rose had created out of the bits and pieces she found on her treasure walks. She had made them with odd items that pleased her, like a meat thermometer, a cell phone, a calculator, a pair of old dentures. One robot had a marble eye that Penny Rose had found in the town graveyard.

Today was Penny Rose's birthday. There would be cake that night. Presents. A few balloons. If you listened very carefully, you'd hear her talking to the robots about it.

"I think having a birthday party with just your parents and your cat is fine. I really do," she told them. "And I have you guys. You're my friends."

She didn't like the way her voice trembled when she said that last part, so she did what she always did when she worried or became upset. She tightened another screw. She loosened a bolt. She changed a battery.

The wind blew across her neck. She shivered and pulled the hood up on her sweatshirt. "Why is it so cold all of a sudden?"

The robots didn't answer.

And maybe it was the force of her determination, or a few stray whiskers from her cat, Arvid, or that northerly wind blowing in through the window that changed every single item in that shed on that cool September afternoon.

Or maybe it was simply a desperate wish from a lonely girl.

Chapter One

The next morning, after a quick visit to the shed, Penny Rose joined her parents at the kitchen table for breakfast. Every Sunday morning since they had moved, her father made pancakes in the shape of insects. He was an entomologist, so he pretty much thought about insects all day.

Penny Rose didn't have the heart to tell him that she hated his pancakes. He was trying very hard to be the family cook now that Mom was busy with her new job at the bank. Besides, Penny Rose liked guessing what the shapes were.

Mom sat at the kitchen table with a lumpy-looking pancake on her plate. She had taken exactly one bite. She looked up when Penny Rose came in and shook her head ever so slightly.

Penny Rose knew what that meant. Another perfectly good batch of pancake batter ruined. He had probably added something "gourmet," like rhubarb or olives. He never seemed to be able to leave pancake batter alone.

Dad slid another lumpy-looking one onto her plate and set it before her.

"Happy Day After Your Birthday!" he said. "I thought I'd make an especially challenging pancake today. See what you think."

Penny Rose stared at the blob of pancake. "Bumblebee?" she asked. She tossed a piece to Arvid, who was the only one who loved Dad's pancakes.

Dad shook his head and turned back to the stove. "Nope. Guess again."

"Oh, I bet it's a beetle!" she said. They had just had a long discussion the day before about beetles.

"Ding, ding, ding! You are correct! Now eat your beetle."

He sat down at the table, smiled at her, and took a bite of his own beetle pancake. He was lanky, like Penny Rose, and had the same black hair and green eyes. He was almost the opposite version of her mother, who had straight blond hair and a stocky build.

"I know you wanted a small birthday party with just us last night," Mom said. "But since we have left-over cake, I thought it might be nice to invite Lark over tonight to help us polish it off."

Penny Rose took a tentative bite of her beetle pancake, which had something odd and crunchy in it. Peanuts? Crackers? She wasn't sure.

"I've said hello to her three times, and she hasn't said one word back to me," Penny Rose said.

"Maybe she's shy," Mom said.

"Or maybe she didn't hear you," Dad said.

"Or maybe she doesn't want to be my friend," Penny Rose said, staring down at her plate.

Penny Rose and her parents had moved to Skillington Avenue twenty-eight days ago, and she had been studying Lark Hinkle from her bedroom window ever since. Lark's house was on the opposite side of the street in the middle of the block. Penny Rose had to crane her neck to get a good vantage point. She could often see Lark standing in her front yard writing notes as she stared through binoculars at the treetops.

Lark was utterly mysterious. She wore enormous sunglasses everywhere, even in their fifth-grade classroom. Sometimes she carried a small metal box.

And Lark didn't seem to have any friends, either. It was so . . . *logical* . . . for her and Penny Rose to be friends, but so far it hadn't happened.

"Besides, it's not like I don't have *any* friends," Penny Rose said. "I have the robots. And Arvid. And you guys."

She looked up from her plate to see her parents giving her the Concerned Stare. They gave her the Concerned Stare when she worked in her shed for long hours or when she talked about how the robots were her friends. They probably worried about other things, too, like flesh-eating viruses and alligators, but Penny Rose knew that approximately 97 percent of their worries had to do with her and how she was adjusting to the new neighborhood.

Given that, she didn't dare mention how when she went into the shed this morning, the air seemed . . . different. Like the cold breeze that had swept in the night before had stayed there. Or how a squirrel with a black smudge on his tail had seemed to follow her as she walked from the house and then watched her from a tree branch the entire time she was in the shed. She was sure if she told them these things, the Concerned Stare would become their permanent expression.

"I think you should go over there and ring her doorbell," Mom said.

"And then just introduce yourself," Dad said. "Ask her if she'd like to see the robots."

"I'll try," Penny Rose said. She took another bite of beetle pancake.

"Great!" Mom said.

Dad smiled and nodded.

First, though, Penny Rose would need a detailed plan. She went up to her bedroom, sat on her bed, and turned on the lamp she had made last year from an olive oil can. A stack of notebooks sat on her nightstand: her New Inventions notebook, her Robot Drawings and Descriptions notebook, and her To-Do List notebook. Her most secret notebook, Conversation Starters, was at the bottom of the pile.

She picked it up, found a clean page, and wrote a quick list of Possible Conversation Starters:

1) "I think binoculars are fun." (Lark seems to like binoculars.)

2) "The sun seems strong today." (Lark often wears sun goop. First determine if the sun does, indeed, seem strong.)

3) "Sunglasses are very wise." (Lark wears sunglasses.)

4) "Do you like robots?" (It is unknown whether or not Lark likes robots, but it is probable that she does since most people do.)

5) "Yesterday was my birthday. Would you like some leftover cake?" (This seems like a good bet, unless she has allergies or is gluten-free or vegan or something.)

6) "What is in that metal box?" (This might be too nosy, although if you're going to carry something so mysterious, you should be prepared for questions.)

Penny Rose looked over her list. She considered what her father said about Lark not hearing her before. She decided she would speak loudly.

Penny Rose tore out the page and tucked it into the tool belt she wore in case she happened upon interesting items for her robots.

"This is it, Arvid," she announced to the small orange cat curled up on her bedroom rug. "This is the day I become friends with Lark Hinkle."

Arvid did what he always did when Penny Rose made important announcements — he yawned.

Chapter Two

Skillington Avenue was unusually quiet. Penny Rose figured that the Gilmore boys who lived next door were making trouble on another street. Bonkers, the mean dog who always barked from the Boilses' front yard, was probably off somewhere slobbering on a ham bone or a small child. Jeremy Boils was up in his room, in front of his computer. She often saw him through his window, and today was no different.

Lark's house was quiet, too. Penny Rose started toward it. Just then, the front door opened.

Lark came out wearing the same sunglasses she wore every day. Instead of her metal box, she carried a grocery bag. She walked down the sidewalk, away from Penny Rose.

This ruined Penny Rose's careful plan. She had planned on walking up to Lark's door and ringing the doorbell. Then she was going to wait until Mrs. Hinkle answered. Then she was going to say, "Hello, is Lark home?"

She had no idea what she was going to do now.

More importantly, where was Lark going?

Lark seemed determined. She was practically speed walking.

Just then, Penny Rose saw something shiny glinting in the middle of the sidewalk.

Penny Rose couldn't help herself when it came to shiny objects. They were inevitably things she could use for her robots—odd bolts and bottle caps and abandoned keys. Once she even found a fork.

She felt herself being pulled toward the shiny object, walking so fast she was almost running. Just before she could reach it, Lark plucked it off the sidewalk.

Penny Rose froze. Her mouth dropped open.

Lark inspected the item before putting it in her bag.

"What is that?" Penny Rose blurted out.

"Just a compass," Lark said. She started walking back to her house. "Nothing you'd be interested in," she called out over her shoulder.

A compass? That would be perfect for her robots! Why did Lark want a compass, anyway?

Penny Rose waited a few moments until Lark went back into her house. She looked up and down the street. No one was there. She checked Jeremy Boils's window. Even he was gone. She crossed Skillington, trying to look like she didn't have a care in the world, and headed toward Lark's house. She stood a foot away from the family of garden gnomes that studded the Hinkles' yard.

Penny Rose crept over to the window that faced the front yard. She crouched behind some overgrown bushes, then slowly stood until she could see inside. Lark walked from one room to another, but that was all she could see.

Penny Rose waited for what seemed like hours. Nothing happened. She sneaked around to the back of the house and flattened herself against the wall. She made sure the backyard was quiet before she peeked around the corner.

And that's when she saw them.

The birdhouses.

Dozens and dozens of them. The entire backyard was bursting with birdhouses.

Not just ordinary birdhouses, either. A pendulum swung from the bottom of one. A flag waved from another's rooftop. One was built like a tiny windmill, its blades spinning in slow circles.

And they were made using all kinds of materials, like plastic buckets and soda cans and tissue boxes.

Lark came out the back door carrying a white birdhouse with a red roof. She had attached the compass to one of its exterior walls. Lark hung it above the bird feeder and tilted her head to one side.

"Nope, not here," she said. She moved it to a higher branch. "That's better."

A bee buzzed near Penny Rose's face. She tried not to move, but when it landed on her nose, she jumped.

"Get away!" she yelled. She swatted at it.

Lark's head swiveled in her direction.

"HEY!" she yelled.

Chapter Three

Penny Rose continued to slap at the bee.

"I, um, I . . ." Beads of sweat popped out on her forehead. "I think binoculars are fun!"

Lark squinted. "What?" Her voice was loud and scratchy.

"The sun is very strong today, isn't it?" Penny Rose was practically shouting as she swatted the bee away with both hands.

Lark frowned. "You're on private property," she said. "And you're spying! And you're acting really weird!"

"I was walking . . ." Penny Rose said. A gushing wave of panic flooded through her body.

"And?"

"I c-c-came here . . ." Penny Rose stammered. She started edging away. She most certainly did not have the appropriate Conversation Starter for this situation. "I walked and I came here—"

"You said that already."

"I have to . . ." Penny Rose didn't finish. Even if she had tried to finish, she wasn't sure what to say to people under normal circumstances, and this was no normal circumstance. *Hello, I was spying on you and saw that you were an excellent birdhouse creator* didn't sound like a very neighborly statement, even though it was truthful.

Penny Rose turned and ran toward the street. She didn't stop running until she got to her shed. From the moment she saw those birdhouses, she knew, she just *knew*, that Lark was like her: she couldn't resist making something from nothing, either.

Once inside the shed, Penny Rose started gathering interesting objects and putting them in her tool belt: a rubber-band ball, a ballpoint pen, a stopwatch.

She looked at her robots on the card table. She had only showed them to her parents, and they had loved them. But that's what parents do—they fawn all over everything their children make. Other kids were different. More discerning. It was possible that Lark may not like them.

"Robots, I need your help."

She sat down at the rickety card table where her robots were lined up. There was iPam, the robot made out of a broken cell phone. Like all the other robots, she had wheels for legs. Her tiny screen had a crack through it, and Penny Rose still hadn't attached both of her antennae arms.

"Nope, not you, iPam," Penny Rose said. "You still need work." She picked up Clunk, whom she had made last week. Clunk's meat-thermometer head was perched on top of an old transistor radio.

"Hmm. Maybe."

The late morning sun glinted off the metal on her meat thermometer. For a second it almost looked like she winked.

"Hello, Fraction." Penny Rose smiled. She was just the robot for the job.

Dear sweet Fraction. The kind calculator with the heart sticker. It was faded now but still distinct on her back.

"You are coming with me," Penny Rose said.

Sharpie, the robot made out of a pencil sharpener and old dentures, kept tipping backward. She wouldn't do.

As Penny Rose picked up Data, a shiver ran through her body. She put her back down quickly.

"That was weird," she murmured.

It was probably her imagination. She had, after all, found Data's marble eye in a cemetery. She was bound to feel a little funny about her.

Actually, everything felt different in her small shed since the cold winds blew through it yesterday. She looked around, taking in the four windows, the dented cardboard box filled with junk in the corner, and the scratched floor.

"What is it?" she whispered.

She finally noticed the five bolts scattered across the table. Five bolts she was certain had not been there before. And a stack of papers on the table was slightly askew. Askew in a way they had not been before.

And it was colder. *Much* colder.

"This is silly," she said to the robots. "I don't have time for this. I'm on a mission." She made a sign with a purple marker and picked up Fraction and Clunk.

"Here we go," she said.

Penny Rose walked around to her front porch and perched Clunk on the top step with the sign she had made. She went down the stairs and checked to see if anyone was watching. She didn't see the Gilmore boys or Jeremy Boils, so she placed the stopwatch in the center of the sidewalk square outside of her house. A few feet from that she placed the rubber-band ball, again right in the center of a square. She crossed the street and placed the ballpoint pen pointing to her house.

Then, on Lark's front doorstep, she propped Fraction up with one arm in the air, as though she were waving hello. Fraction was, in Penny Rose's opinion, an extremely friendly robot, what with her heart sticker.

The next part of her plan was the trickiest.

Penny Rose bent down low as she tiptoed over to Lark's doorbell. She poked it once — hard — and dashed toward her house as fast as she could, jumping over the ballpoint pen, over the rubber-band ball, over the stopwatch, until she got to the bushes next to her house's front steps. She crouched down behind the fattest bush and waited.

She waited and watched. Her knees ached. Her mouth turned dry and sticky. In the distance she

heard the Gilmore boys charge out their back door and into their yard. If they found her interesting items first, her plan would be ruined.

Penny Rose cautiously peered out of the bushes. She saw Lark pick up the ballpoint pen and put it in her pocket. She was holding Fraction.

Lark crossed the street slowly, following Penny Rose's trail. After she picked up the rubber-band ball and stopwatch, she straightened up and stared right at Clunk. She paused, her head tilted to one side. She picked up the sign Penny Rose had made and read it out loud.

"I like your birdhouses. Would you like to help make a home for my robots?"

Lark frowned. She looked up and saw Penny Rose watching her from behind the bush.

"Let's see these robots of yours."

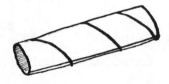

Chapter Four

Penny Rose climbed out from behind the bushes.

"OK," she said. "I can, um, take you . . ."

She let her sentence trail off as she led Lark, holding both Fraction and Clunk now, to the shed. She pushed the door open and motioned Lark inside.

"I made this one out of a pencil sharpener and, um, dentures," she said, walking over to the card table. She reached down and turned on Sharpie. Her heart beat quickly as Sharpie moved a few inches forward on the card table and then stopped. "They still need . . . um . . . work and . . . stuff."

Lark put Fraction and Clunk down on the table with the other robots. She stood with her hands on her hips and stared at them.

She didn't say anything. Not one word.

Penny Rose's hands shook as she turned on each of the robots.

"This is a marble I found in the Calvary Graveyard," she said, pointing to Data's one pink eye. She flipped Data's switch. The eye spun once, then stopped.

"I made this one from a cell phone."

When Penny Rose picked up iPam, her one antenna arm fell off. An ant crawled across her cracked screen. Penny Rose should have made them all perfect first. This was no way to show them to a possible new friend.

"And, well, you saw the other two — Clunk and Fraction."

Penny Rose held her breath. She couldn't help but look at the robots through Lark's eyes, and now they all seemed like . . . junk. She nervously picked up Fraction and punched in 1 + 1 in the calculator.

"See, she's really just a calculator. They're just, I don't know, silly things I made. That's all," Penny Rose said. She glanced at Lark. It was impossible to tell what she was thinking while wearing those dark glasses.

Before Penny Rose could say another word, Lark was gone. She could hear her closing the gate to the backyard.

"That was weird," Penny Rose said.

The squirrel with the black smudge on his tail chattered at her from his perch on a branch.

Penny Rose looked into his small black eyes.

"I guess she thought they were dumb," she said to him.

The squirrel flicked his tail at her, as if he agreed with Lark's assessment, and scurried into the bushes.

It had been a mistake bringing Lark here. She would probably tell everyone at school that Penny Rose was a weirdo with ugly handmade robots in a moldy old shed.

She flopped down onto her chair and sighed. She obviously hadn't thought this through. It was too late now. She was destined to be friendless.

Penny Rose jumped at the sound of the back gate's creak. She got up and looked out the window. Lark was heading back to the shed with two large bags. She walked into the shed as though she had been coming there all her life and unloaded the contents of her bags onto the floor.

"I have all these lava lamps," she said, taking out a few strange-looking conical shaped lamps. "I haven't been able to figure out how to use them as birdhouses, but as I was looking around, I thought they might make a good forest." She straightened up and looked at Penny Rose. "Do you have electricity out here?"

Penny Rose stared at Lark for a moment before motioning to the corner of the room.

"Over there," she said.

Lark brought a lamp over to the power strip and plugged it in.

"Perfect!" Lark said. "Let's plug in all of them."

Penny Rose helped her until every single lava lamp was lit. The two girls watched silently as the colorful globs inside the lava lamps floated up and down.

"It looks like a robot forest," Penny Rose said quietly. She almost thought she could hear the robots cheering.

"I also brought this," Lark said. She took her metal box out of one of the bags.

Penny Rose leaned closer. She held her breath as Lark opened the mysterious box. This was the box Penny Rose had been curious about since the first time she saw Lark.

"So I like to bird-watch, and I like birds. I feed them, and I make them houses." She paused and looked at

Penny Rose carefully. She took a breath. "Sometimes they bring me presents."

"Oh," Penny Rose said.

Lark reached into the box and picked out a key. The top of it was painted pale blue. "This is one of my favorites," she said. "I remember when I saw a crow carrying this in its beak. He dropped it right in the middle of my backyard."

"Really?" Penny Rose couldn't help but frown. It didn't seem plausible that ordinary birds would bring presents to a ten-year-old girl, but then nothing about Lark was ordinary.

"Yes, he did," Lark said. "I use all these things to make my birdhouses. Sometimes I have to travel a bit to find new stuff, but mostly I use what they drop into my yard."

"Huh," said Penny Rose.

"You said you wanted a home for the robots," Lark said.

"I think they could use one."

"I don't think they need a home at all," Lark said.

Penny Rose inhaled sharply. "Oh, but I thought—"

"What they really need," Lark said, "is a *metropolis*."

"Most definitely!" Penny Rose said. "That is *exactly* what they need."

"I have tons of stuff from the birds," Lark said. She dug through her box and brought out a small plastic bag. "They've brought me all kinds of coins. We could use them in the metropolis. Or this," she said, holding up another bag. "This is filled with paper clips. We could bend them into—I don't know—something."

Penny Rose looked at Lark and smiled. Lark smiled back. A big toothy smile.

"Do you like birthday cake?" Penny Rose asked.

"Who doesn't?"

"Wait here."

Penny Rose ran back to her house and put two slices of birthday cake and two forks on a tray. She ran up to her bedroom, tucked her Robot notebook under her arm, and hurried back to the shed. She and Lark ate and planned and planned and ate until it was time for Lark to go home.

It was possibly the best Day After Her Birthday Penny Rose had ever had.

That afternoon, just as she was about to leave the shed, she smiled at all the robots.

"Looks like I have a friend after all," she said.

As she was turning to leave, she heard a strange whirring behind her. She spun around, but all she could see were the robots lined up on the table.

"Must have been the wind," she said. She stepped through the doorway.

When she heard the whirring again, she decided not to turn around. It was only the wind. She was sure of it.

Chapter Five

The next few days were quite miraculous for Penny Rose.

She and Lark were now friends, which made Penny Rose dizzy with happiness. They sat together on the bus and ate their lunch together every day. Lark even let Penny Rose have half of her lunch when Penny Rose's dad had made something especially weird, like the tomato and pickle sandwich he once packed. After school they went to the shed and worked on their robot metropolis.

They even liked the same snack—cinnamon raisin toast with creamy peanut butter.

Of course no friend was perfect. Penny Rose knew this. And Lark was definitely a bit odd. Kids sometimes made faces behind her back when she stood at the edge of the playground and stared at the trees through her binoculars. Penny Rose pretended not to notice the other kids and would sit on a swing until Lark was finished bird-watching, and they would walk back to their classroom together.

Lark wasn't afraid to let her weirdness show, and Penny Rose thought that was very brave.

As if having a new best friend weren't miraculous enough, on Thursday Penny Rose found a mysterious envelope tucked into the vents in her locker. Inside the envelope was a note written in green ink on notebook paper.

> We are the Secret Science Society. We think you might be a good member, but first you need to pass some tests. Please put an everyday household item that uses a mineral into this envelope. Put the envelope underneath Webster's Dictionary in the library. Don't let anyone see you.
>
> If you use Google to help with this, we will know.
>
> You have until tomorrow morning.

Don't tell anyone about this note. Not even your mother. We are a <u>secret</u> society.

Sincerely,

The Secret Science Society

Was this for real? Or was it a mean joke?

Penny Rose looked up and down the hallway. Merry Zwack and Lily Proom, two popular girls, were whispering to each other. The Fantini twins were flipping through their notebooks. Pete Smithers, the biggest boy in class, was playing hacky sack while his best friend, Jose Goldbloom, loudly cheered him on. No one was paying any attention to Penny Rose.

If it was a joke, kids would be watching her and snickering. No one was watching her at all.

She reread the note, folded it up, and put it in her backpack.

There was no doubt in her mind that she would do what the note asked. She knew exactly what to put in the envelope. She and her parents had gone to the Museum of Science and Industry this past summer, and there had been a display all about rocks and minerals. Penny Rose spent so much time there that her mom had bought her a book about minerals from the gift shop.

Penny Rose put a pencil in the envelope, shut her locker, and race-walked down the hall to the library. She paused outside the door and wrote on the outside of the envelope:

Graphite is a mineral, and it's in pencils.

She peeked inside. Lark was at the librarian's desk, checking out books.

Was Lark part of the Secret Science Society? It didn't seem likely. Lark was not the kind of girl who would willingly be part of any club. She was, in fact, about as anti-club as you could get. But, more importantly, Penny Rose was the only kid at school Lark liked.

Penny Rose's heart pounded as she walked as casually as possible to the dictionary.

Lark turned and saw her. "What's up?" she asked.

"Just looking up a word," Penny Rose said. She flipped open the huge dictionary.

"Oh, OK," Lark said. She turned back to Ms. Codell, the librarian, and started talking about the latest book she had read on birds.

If Lark was part of the Secret Science Society, she would have known what Penny Rose was doing. She would have given her a secret look, as if to say, "Hey, I know what you're doing by the dictionary!"

But Lark didn't do that. She didn't seem suspicious about what Penny Rose was doing at all.

Still, Penny Rose didn't want to take any chances. She flipped through the dictionary's pages. While Ms. Codell checked out Lark's books, Penny Rose quickly placed the envelope under the dictionary.

"Got it," Penny Rose said, turning around to face Lark.

"What was the word?" Lark asked.

Penny Rose stopped breathing for a moment.

"I forget."

Lark laughed. "You're so funny! Come on, let's line up for the bus."

Once they were on the bus, Lark settled in next to Penny Rose and opened up her bird-watching notebook.

"I decided today that crows are definitely my favorite kind of bird," she said in her loud, scratchy voice. Lily Proom and Merry Zwack turned around in their seats to look at her. Pete Smithers shot her a mean look. Jeremy Boils got up with a huff and moved one seat away from them.

"For one thing, crows are super smart. Also? I think they are beautiful, and so does my grandma on my mother's side, Oma Maud. Mom doesn't like them

as much since a crow swooped down really close to Finn once when he was in the backyard, and he cried for, like, hours. So now he hates birds, which is weird since he's my brother, you know?" She took a deep breath. "You wanna go bird-watching sometime?" she asked.

Penny Rose had been trying to pay attention to Lark, but it was hard. All she could think about was the note. She couldn't figure out how the Secret Science Society knew about her love of science. It was true that she had aced the first science test, and that Mr. Moyes had made a big deal about how she was the only one who got the question about the earth's atmosphere right. And she had won a statewide science competition the year before and had had her name in the local newspaper. That was in her old hometown, though. How did they know about that?

"Hello? Penny Rose? Do you want to bird-watch with me sometime?"

Penny Rose snapped to attention. "Um, yeah, sure," she said, although, if she was being completely honest with herself, it didn't sound nearly as much fun as being part of a secret science society.

Chapter Six

On Friday Penny Rose practically ran to her locker. She opened it slowly, ready to catch the note from the Secret Science Society in case it fell out. Her heart thumped against her ribs. It had to be there. It *had* to.

She took every notebook out and shook each one. Gently at first. Then she shook them all again frantically.

Nothing.

No note anywhere.

She was sure she had done everything right. And she knew graphite was a mineral.

She slammed her locker shut.

It must have been a joke. Her cheeks burned hotter than a Bunsen burner. She didn't dare look around.

Of course it could have been a mistake. Maybe right now some kid was kicking himself for putting the note in the wrong locker.

Yes, that was probably it.

It was so very silly, really, to get excited over a note. She had a new best friend and the beginnings of a great robot metropolis, roboTown. That was enough.

She and Lark worked on roboTown every day for the next two weeks. Penny Rose almost forgot about the note.

Lark came over to Penny Rose's house early in the morning the Saturday before Columbus Day carrying a Macy's shopping bag. They would have three whole days to work in the shed, and they wanted to make the most of it.

"I found these in the basement," she said, pulling a tangle of Christmas lights out of the bag. "Mom said I could use them."

Along the top of the walls of the shed were hooks that probably once held rakes and shovels. These hooks, Lark had pointed out, were just right for hanging Christmas lights.

"Great!" Penny Rose said. "Let's go!"

As soon as they walked into the shed, they saw it.

"What happened to the fence?" Lark asked.

Penny Rose shook her head.

Ever since Penny Rose's birthday, strange things had been happening in the shed. They were small at first. One morning iPam's arms were raised. Another time the tin-can elevator in roboTown was up instead of down. She and Lark had wondered each time if they were misremembering. Did *they* put Clunk at the top of the slide the day before? Did *they* leave Sharpie standing in the corner facing the wall?

But today the fence was knocked down. It was more than two feet long and consisted of fourteen Popsicle sticks and twelve pebbles. They knew they didn't do that.

"Do you think animals got in?" Lark asked as she picked up the Popsicle sticks. She blew on her hands to warm them.

"I don't think so," Penny Rose said. "The door was closed."

"It's so weird how these things keep happening," Lark said. "Maybe we should stay up one night and spy."

"Or we could do some kind of video surveillance, like my mom has at the bank."

"Oooh, that's a good idea," Lark said. "We could be modern-day Nancy Drews."

Penny Rose considered the facts as she helped Lark pick up the Popsicle sticks. Something was definitely going on. The temperature in the shed dropped each day, even though the outside weather was warm and balmy for October. Sometimes, when everything outside was quiet, inside she could hear a low humming. And when Penny Rose walked into the shed these days, the hairs on her arms and the back of her neck stood up.

Penny Rose tried to think of scientific explanations for all of it, but nothing fit. So she pushed the thoughts into the bottom drawer of her brain and kept quiet.

Despite the odd happenings, roboTown was everything Penny Rose had hoped it would be thanks to Lark. A sign hung above the town. It spelled out *roboTown* in small lightbulbs that had been screwed into a piece of plywood painted electric blue. Stacked shoe boxes, gift boxes, and wooden crates made up the buildings, which were, in places, as tall as Penny Rose. There were ramps made from toy train tracks that went from one level to the next, as well as a bright pink slide that was originally made for her Barbie dolls. Some rooms were

divided by sheets of pennies sandwiched between clear contact paper. One room had bubble-wrap wallpaper and a paper-clip chandelier. The battery-operated elevator made out of a soup can was one of her favorite parts of the town, along with the coffee table made from an old MP3 player.

Penny Rose turned on the Lava Lamp Forest. In front of it was the obstacle course they had built for the robots made of toilet-paper tubes, springs, spools of thread, and thumbtacks.

Lark told Penny Rose that some of the items they used to make roboTown were gifts from the birds, like the three-cent stamp and the green ribbon. Penny Rose would simply nod. She wasn't quite sure what to believe when it came to Lark and her bird stories.

Lark climbed onto one of the chairs. "Hand me a string," she said.

Penny Rose untangled a string of lights and handed it to her. Something scratched at one of the window screens.

Chimney. Of course.

When Lark first saw the squirrel with the black smudge on his tail, she decided he needed a name.

"His tail looks like it was dragged through some soot," she had said. Penny Rose thought it was the perfect name for the odd squirrel.

"So I was thinking that for Halloween we could both be robots," Lark said. "We could make our costumes out of old boxes and use silver paint and stick all sorts of things onto the boxes, like dials and tubes. What do you think?"

Penny Rose loved the idea of dressing up in the same costume for Halloween. It was something best friends did, and it was better than anything she could ever think of. Maybe even better than becoming a member of the Secret Science Society.

"We'll be Best Friend Robots!" she said.

"Halloween is coming up! We better get to work on them soon," Lark said.

They stayed in the shed fussing with the lights and the ramps and the paper-clip chandelier until the sunlight dimmed. Finally, after they had hung the last string of lights, Lark got off her chair and took a step back.

"Let's see how they look," she said, dusting her palms together.

Penny Rose flicked the switch. The strings lit up like a city skyline.

Lark clapped. "I LOVE IT!" she yelled.

They stared at it until they heard Penny Rose's mom calling to them from the back door.

"Lark, your mother wants you home. It's almost time for your dinner," she said. "Penny Rose, time for you to come in now, too."

"OK!" Lark and Penny Rose called back in unison.

Penny Rose unplugged the lights before leaving the shed.

"It's getting too cold to work in here anyway," said Lark.

"It is," Penny Rose agreed, rubbing her hands together.

"Bye, robots," they both said. Lark gave Penny Rose a quick wave before going home.

Penny Rose went straight to the kitchen to wash her hands. She stood in the middle of the kitchen wiping them off with a dish towel when she heard a thump of footsteps on the porch, then a rustle by the front door. She walked into the front hall and watched as a green envelope slipped through the mail slot.

The mail carrier always came at noon, so whatever was in that envelope wasn't ordinary mail. Penny Rose cautiously picked it up. Her name was scrawled across the front. She opened it. The note inside was written with the same green ink.

You passed your first test. Now you must make something that is extremely science-y. Once you have made it, text a picture and a description to this number: 847-555-0190.
Sincerely,
The Secret Science Society

Penny Rose pushed open the front door and stood on the porch. She looked up and down the street. It was empty. Whoever had put the note through the mail slot was long gone.

Or hiding.

She had the distinct feeling that someone was watching her.

Chapter Seven

That night Penny Rose couldn't fall asleep. Every time she got close, she would have a new exciting thought about the Secret Science Society, and her eyes would pop open.

The fact that they had a cell phone that wasn't just for emergencies fascinated her. She didn't have one. Maybe the Secret Science Society had a *secret* cell phone. That was even better.

They probably had some kind of secret handshake, too.

And a secret language.

She spent a few minutes worrying about how she would text them. She'd need to use her mom's phone and then delete everything afterward. She also worried she would not be able to learn the secret language. She was not very good in Spanish, and that wasn't even secret.

She also didn't know what to show them. The robots seemed like the obvious choice, but she wasn't sure that was a good idea.

But the most important question of all was, *Who was in the Secret Science Society?*

Penny Rose flipped and flopped. Finally she switched on her bedside lamp. Arvid blinked.

"Sorry," she said to him. "Just can't sleep." She got out of bed and walked over to her desk.

"This deserves a new notebook," she said. She rummaged through her desk until she found an empty one. On the cover she wrote: POSSIBLE SECRET SOCIETY MEMBERS. She knew that they had to be in her school, and they were probably in her class. She wrote down a list of her classmates and everything she knew about them.

> Lark Hinkle — best friend, does not seem particularly interested in anything other than birds and roboTown

Lily Proom — wears cool purple boots, has the
best hair in all of fifth grade
Pete Smithers — feet the size of watermelons,
makes lots of fart jokes
Jose Goldbloom — best friends with Pete,
laughs too hard at Pete's fart jokes,
nose-picker
Max and Jack Fantini — skinny, quiet, never
talk to anyone but each other
Jeremy Boils — owns the meanest dog on
earth, seems mad all the time, has never
said one word to me
Britta Rosen — talks about dragons, writes stories
about dragons, and wears dragon T-shirts
Michael Yoo — stares out the window all day,
never raises his hand, hums a lot
Laticia Washington — complains about home-
work all the time, draws pictures of ponies
instead of taking notes
Sarah Stew — sits in the front row and keeps
her hand up all through class, even if the
teacher hasn't asked anything
Dale Grimes — always has crumbs in the
corner of his mouth, smells like pea soup

Alfonso Segreti — best athlete in school, very
    popular, good at math
Merry Zwack — best soccer player in school,
    did an amazing video on global warming,
    wears blue rubber bands in her braces

Penny Rose went through the list and wound up crossing off every single name. Some kids were too popular for something as geeky as a science club, like Merry Zwack and Alfonso Segreti. Others were too shy to want to be part of a club, like Max and Jack Fantini. Others, like Jose Goldbloom, didn't have any interest in science. And some, like Jeremy Boils, seemed to actively dislike her, so she doubted they'd invite her to join a club.

Maybe someone from a strange out-of-town science club had sneaked into her school to deliver the first note. Somehow this person disguised himself or herself as a student and tucked the note into Penny Rose's locker without anyone noticing.

It was an exciting thought, but Penny Rose doubted it.

Penny Rose yawned. She put down her pen and stared out her bedroom window.

And that's when she saw it.

Something flashed in her yard, like a light had been switched on for a second.

But there were no lights in her yard. In fact, the only things in her yard were the old shed, a clump of overgrown bushes, a few fir trees, a bird feeder, and a hose.

Penny Rose got up and walked over to the window. She half expected to see a burglar with a flashlight, but the yard, which was dimly lit by the moon, was empty.

She kept staring out her window until her eyeballs felt dry and itchy with the effort. Nothing happened. Could the flash have come from the Gilmores' yard, or —

It flashed again. But this time she saw exactly where it came from.

Inside the shed.

She was sure of it. The Christmas lights in the shed had been switched on for just a second. Someone was in there.

It couldn't be Lark. Although they had talked about spying on the shed, she would have told Penny Rose if she had decided to do that. She would have no reason to go in there by herself at night.

No, Lark wouldn't go into the shed at such an odd hour without her.

It flashed again. Twice. Someone was in her shed!

Someone was trespassing! *And they were trespassing in her shed! With her robots!*

Penny Rose stuffed her feet into her slippers. She pulled a sweater over her pajamas and tiptoed toward the hall.

"Shhh," she said to Arvid. "No meowing." She pulled her door closed.

Her parents' bedroom light was off. She tiptoed down the stairs, grabbed a flashlight from the front hall closet, and slipped out the back door.

She stood just outside the doorway, staring at the shed. A cold breeze ruffled the hair around her face. She squinted, but the shed looked as empty as ever. She knew what she saw, though. Someone, or something, was in her shed.

Penny Rose gripped the flashlight and walked across the yard slowly until she was only a few inches away from the door. All was silent except for the rustle of leaves. Then she heard a floorboard squeak from inside the shed. She took a deep breath and turned the doorknob.

Penny Rose stood motionless until her eyes adjusted to the dark. She could see something moving in the corner.

Just then the Christmas lights turned on again and stayed on. Clunk was standing by the outlet. She had the plug between her antennae arms. She pulled the plug out, and the lights winked out once more.

As if in a dream, Penny Rose went over to the plug, bent down, and took it gently out of Clunk's arms. Her hands shook as she plugged the lights back in. Penny Rose stared at Clunk for a moment before picking her up.

Clunk's ON/OFF button was positioned at OFF. What was happening?

Penny Rose flicked her switch on and off and put her back down. Clunk immediately zoomed over to the Christmas lights and unplugged them.

"But your switch is off! How are you doing that?"

She had also not programmed Clunk to use her arms that way, and yet there she was, unplugging the Christmas lights. Penny Rose reached down and plugged them in once again.

Penny Rose straightened up and looked around. This was not possible. She must be dreaming.

A square of blue light in the corner caught her eye. It was iPam. The small screen on her belly glowed. iPam moved toward her slowly on her toy-car wheels. Penny Rose held her breath as she watched iPam approach.

There were words on her screen.

A *text*, to be precise. Penny Rose knelt down next to her and read it out loud:

HELLO, PENNI ROSE.

Chapter Eight

The next morning's air was damp and cool. Penny Rose shivered in front of the shed's door. Every muscle in her body was tense as she listened for the sound of the robots' movements.

What had happened the night before was strange. Part of her was frightened of what she had seen. But a larger part of her was thrilled. If it was real — if her robots did come alive — it meant that she, Penny Rose Mooney, had created artificial intelligence!

She thought she heard a tiny *thump* from inside the shed.

The night before, after reading iPam's text, Penny Rose had slowly backed out of the shed. As soon as she was in the yard, she raced to the back door, yanked it open, dashed up the stairs as quietly as possible, and hopped into bed with a startled Arvid. She pulled the covers over her head and curled up into a ball. Breathing heavily, she went over and over what had happened and came to the same conclusion each time. The robots had moved on their own, and iPam had texted her. It seemed scientifically impossible.

She hadn't slept at all.

Now, as she was standing in front of the shed in the early morning sun, she could definitely hear a faint whirring noise. She opened the door wide enough to poke her head in.

Everything was still for a moment. Then Clunk spun in a circle. She waved.

Penny Rose gingerly stepped inside.

Sharpie rolled into a corner and stared at the wall. Fraction zoomed over to her and tapped on her sneaker.

"You're alive," she whispered hoarsely, picking Fraction up. She punched in 1 + 1 on the calculator and got 2. Fraction was the same as always, and yet very, very different. After Penny Rose set her back down, she did a quick spin before joining Sharpie by the wall.

iPam's screen flashed.

GOOD MORNING.

"H-h-hi," Penny Rose stammered.

The back door slammed. Penny Rose jumped.

"Penny Rose! Lark's on the phone!" Mom called.

Lark! Of course! She had to tell Lark! After all, Lark had spent almost as much time with the robots as Penny Rose had. She would want to know this important development. She and Penny Rose were a team.

"OK!" Penny Rose called back. "See you guys in a second," she said before racing out of the shed. Once she was in the house, she grabbed the phone Mom held out to her.

"Hey," she said.

"Hi there! What are you—"

"Can you come over?" Penny Rose said quickly.

"OK," Lark said. "I was going to bring—"

Penny Rose interrupted her before she could go into a long monologue. "Great," she said. "See you soon."

She hung up the phone and dashed past her puzzled mom. She bounced up and down on her tiptoes in front of the shed as she waited.

Lark strolled through the back gate minutes later.

"What's the rush? Why did you hang up the phone like that?"

"It's the robots," Penny Rose whispered, waving Lark closer.

"What about them?"

"They came alive last night."

Lark snorted. "Very funny."

"I'm serious," Penny Rose said.

"Come on."

"I'm not kidding you," Penny Rose said. "They really did! iPam even texted me. Twice now. They were still alive this morning, and they're zooming around in the shed!"

Lark looked right into Penny Rose's eyes. Penny Rose stared back without flinching.

"You're not kidding," Lark said.

Penny Rose shook her head. "No."

Lark took a deep breath. "OK, let's go in, then."

Penny Rose turned the knob and pushed open the door. She and Lark stood in the doorway.

A sliver of sunlight stretched across the floor. The light bounced off of iPam and Clunk, but they didn't move.

Penny Rose scanned the shed. Fraction was in the corner with Sharpie. Data stood by the slide. None of them moved.

"It's just Lark," Penny Rose said. "You guys can move around now."

They didn't stir.

"Come on, you guys!" Penny Rose said. "Move! Text! Do something!"

A wave of prickly heat spread across Penny Rose's chest and face. A piece of paper on the card table fluttered for a moment in the breeze, but that was it. "Come on, move!" she yelled.

The stillness in the shed mocked her. She stormed over to iPam and picked her up. "She sent me a text last night! It said, 'Hello, Penni Rose'! She misspelled my name and everything! And she sent another one this morning!" Penny Rose held iPam close to her face and pleaded with her. "Please, please talk to me! Send me a text!"

But iPam was as cold and lifeless in her hand as an old mug. She put her back down on the floor.

"I don't get it," Penny Rose said. "They were moving just this morning! Maybe if you go outside and come back in suddenly—"

Lark shrugged. "OK," she said. She left the shed.

As soon as she left, Penny Rose crouched down on the floor. "Come on, you guys, it's OK to move. I promise!"

The robots stayed in their places.

"Please? Pleeease?" Penny Rose begged. She shifted into a cross-legged position and sat very still.

Nothing happened.

Lark came back into the shed. She looked down at Penny Rose on the floor.

"I know this sounds impossible," Penny Rose said. Her voice shook, and she could feel the tips of her ears burning. "But you have to believe me. They were alive last night. They really were."

Lark came over and sat next to Penny Rose. "I believe you," she said quietly. She put her arm around Penny Rose's shoulders. "You are my very best friend, and I know you would never lie to me. If you say they moved, they moved."

"Really?" Penny Rose asked. Her eyes filled with tears. She looked down and brushed them away.

"Really. They probably just aren't in the mood or something."

The sun warmed Penny Rose's back. She let out a shaky sigh.

"Thanks," she said.

Penny Rose saw something flash out of the corner of her eye. She slowly turned her head.

iPam's screen was lit up.

One by one, the other robots moved.

"Oh, my gosh . . ." Lark whispered.

Data rolled over to Clunk, who spun in slow circles, then stopped. Sharpie's dentures clacked together. Fraction used the tin-can elevator to get to the top of roboTown and then rolled down the slide.

iPam wheeled herself over to the girls.

WELCOME, LARK! HOW R U?

"Hey, you," Lark said. A huge smile spread across her face. "Took you long enough."

"Yeah," Penny Rose said, wiping a stray tear off her cheek. "Sure did!"

They watched in awe for hours as the robots zipped around the obstacle course, slid down the slide, and rode in the tin-can elevator. Every once in a while, iPam texted them with a brief LOL or WOOT! When dinnertime rolled around, Lark sighed.

"Guess I'd better go," she said.

"Yeah, me, too," Penny Rose said.

As soon as she said that, the robots stopped what they were doing to gather in a tight circle. They beeped and waved their antennae arms.

"What's going on?" Lark asked.

"I have no idea," Penny Rose said. "Looks like they're discussing something important, though."

Finally, iPam rolled up to them on her toy-car wheels.

WE WOULD LIKE A PET PLEASE.

Lark and Penny Rose looked at each other and shrugged.

"OK, then," Lark said. "We'll see what we can do."

Chapter Nine

The next day at school crawled by. Penny Rose and Lark thought it was too risky to talk about the pet for the robots with so many kids nearby, so they waited until they got off the bus to discuss it.

"How are we going to get them a pet?" Lark asked. "Could we bring Arvid into the shed?"

"You're too allergic," Penny Rose said. The few times that Arvid had brushed up against Lark had brought on sneezing attacks.

"We'll keep thinking," Lark said.

The robots greeted them with beeps and flashes of light as soon as they walked through the door.

"This is a dream come true," Lark said. "It's even better than bird-watching."

"But how is this happening?" Penny Rose asked. "I've gone over it a thousand times, but I still don't understand it."

"It's magic."

"Magic?" Penny Rose frowned. "I don't know about that."

Robots, she knew, could do all sorts of things, like play chess and drive cars. It was possible that she had added just the right component, and that component made them act this way. She just wished she knew what that one component was.

"Well, whatever it is, we really do need to keep all of this secret," Lark said. "We can't have anyone find out about them. Right?"

Penny Rose didn't say anything. iPam rolled over to her and tapped her shoe.

GOOD AFTERNOON. HOPE YOU ARE WELL. FYI BTW, IT'S TOO DARK AT NIGHT.

"Oh, OK," Penny Rose said. "We can get you a night-light. I think there's one in the kitchen. I'll plug it in before we leave."

LOL. THX. AND WE LIKE PENNIES.

"Pennies? I guess I have some," Penny Rose said.

DO NOT FORGET WE'D LIKE A PET. FYI. THX.

"We know, but that's going to be a little tougher," Penny Rose said.

"Hello? Penny Rose?" Lark leaned across the wobbly card table and looked Penny Rose in the eye. "We need to have some kind of formal thing that says we can't talk about the robots to anyone," Lark said.

Penny Rose felt iPam tap on her shoe again.

RUBBER BANDS ARE FUN, BTW.

"OK, OK," Penny Rose said.

"OK to what?" Lark asked. "Me or iPam?"

"Both. Let's get their stuff first."

Penny Rose got up from her chair and rummaged around in the big box in the corner until she found a pad of paper and a pen. "What else do you need, iPam?"

Penny Rose wrote as quickly as she could while iPam texted what she wanted. Minutes later she showed the list to Lark.

Night-light	Buttons	Double-sided
Rubber bands	Pennies	tape
Stickers	Paper clips	

"What if I take the first three items and you take the rest?"

Lark looked over the list. "Got it."

By the time Penny Rose got back to the shed with the items iPam had asked for, Lark was dumping out the buttons, pennies, paper clips, and double-sided tape from her pockets.

"Oh, and here!" she said, smiling. She dug a silver hoop earring out of her pocket and put it in the middle of the floor. "A little something from the birds."

The robots buzzed and beeped their appreciation. Lark bowed before sitting in her chair.

"The thing is, if people know about them, they'll want to examine them and take them apart," Lark said, picking up where she had left off. "They won't realize it's magic."

"But what if it's science?" Penny Rose asked. She went over to the outlet and plugged in the night-light.

"They'll still want to take them away and, like, experiment on them," Lark said. "Do you really want strangers taking them apart?"

"No, definitely not," Penny Rose said. There were times when she was nervous watching Lark handle the robots. She couldn't imagine having a stranger handle them. "We could do a ritual," Lark said, jumping up from her chair. "We could cut our fingers and mix our blood together!"

"Ew, no!"

Lark looked up at the ceiling. "OK, how about we sign an oath. We swear to keep it to just us. No dweebs, doofuses, or dorks." She smiled one of her huge toothy smiles. "That will be how it starts! No dweebs, doofuses, or dorks!"

She picked up the pad that Penny Rose had made the list on and started writing.

THE PROCLAMATION:
Lark Hinkle and Penny Rose Mooney do hereby proclaim that we will not allow any dweebs, doofuses, or dorks to see our robots. Parental Type People must be kept in the dark as much as possible AND they can never, ever know that the robots are alive. The robots are a secret and are not meant for the general public. We do solemnly swear that we will always keep this secret until the day we die, and even after that.
    Sincerely,
    Lark Hinkle and Penny Rose Mooney

She signed and dated it, then pushed the pad over to Penny Rose to sign.

Penny Rose hesitated. Keeping the robots a secret until the day she died seemed like an awfully big promise. What if her robots could help the blind or create a force field that blocked head lice from hopping onto kids' heads?

Or help a certain someone get into a certain secret science club?

Lark nudged the pad closer to Penny Rose. "Come on! We need to do this. We need to make sure they stay safe. Look at them!"

Penny Rose looked down. Clunk was pulling the Christmas lights' plug in and out of the wall again. Fraction chased iPam through the obstacle course. Sharpie stood in the corner gnashing her teeth. Data gazed out the window from the highest point of roboTown, her marble eye turning slowly.

They were so small. So easily broken. And they seemed so very happy.

She pulled the pad closer and signed and dated on the line Lark had drawn.

Something scratched at the screen in the window.

"Hi, Chimney," Penny Rose said.

Chimney scratched again.

"Hey," Lark said excitedly. "They wanted a pet, right?"

"Yes . . ."

"How about Chimney?"

"I don't know," Penny Rose said. "You think so?"

"Let's ask!" Lark said. "iPam, what about that squirrel? Do you think—"

Before Lark could finish her sentence, iPam replied: YES. MOST DEFINITELY. YES!

"Let's try it!" Lark said.

"Gosh, I'm not sure, Lark . . ."

But Lark hurried over to the door and opened it just enough to let a small squirrel in if he was so inclined. She stepped away from the door quickly and sat back down in her chair.

"Let's see if he takes the hint," Lark said. "I wish we had some food or something."

They watched the door.

"Maybe he won't come in," Penny Rose said.

"Maybe he will."

Even the robots waited. They stopped all movement and faced the door.

Finally, Chimney made his way into the shed with surprisingly slow, cautious movements.

Penny Rose held her breath. What if he went wild and they couldn't get him out? What if he bit one of the robots? Or her?

Data and iPam rolled over to him on their tiny wheels. They petted his bushy tail and stroked his back. Chimney blinked, but that was all. Soon all the robots were crowded around Chimney, beeping and flashing.

"Phew!" Penny Rose said. "That was kind of cool and kind of nerve-racking."

"Most definitely," Lark said, smiling. "I guess this whole time all Chimney wanted was to come in and play with the robots."

Lark shook her head.

"Wow," she whispered. "Real live robots and their pet squirrel. It's like weird on top of weird, squared."

Chapter Ten

Penny Rose and Lark decided that the walls of the shed needed color. Penny Rose's mom and dad had painted the kitchen a few weeks before and had extra paint, so the next day the two girls got into old clothes after school and brought the cans of paint and paintbrushes out to the shed. Chimney waited by the door.

"Well, look who's here!" Lark said. "He's waiting by the door like a dog!"

"Come on in, Chimney!" Penny Rose said, holding the door open for him.

The girls gasped as soon as they walked into the shed.

"What is going on?" Lark asked.

The robots zoomed up to them with buttons and pennies taped to their small metal bodies. Around their necks were stacks of colorful rubber bands. Each one also wore a button hat. And draped all over roboTown were strings of paper-clip garlands. Clunk rolled over to Chimney and put the silver hoop earring on top of his head.

"What are you doing?" Penny Rose asked. iPam answered:

WE'RE HAVING A PARTY.

"You guys are too funny!" Lark said, laughing. "We're going to make everything even more festive with this yellow paint."

She started opening up paint cans. "It's so sunny and cheerful and reminds me of canaries. Canaries aren't my favorite bird or anything, but we had one when I was little and he was pretty cool. We named him Lemon. When he died, I downloaded this song called 'Yellow Bird,' and we played it while I read a poem I had written about birds."

Penny Rose was only half listening. As she painted, her mind wandered to the proclamation. Was showing the Secret Science Society her robots really going against it? It would just be a picture after all.

"Look, they're staring at us!" Lark said.

Behind them stood the robots. They stared at the two girls without beeping or whirring.

"It's like this is the most fascinating thing in the world to them!" Penny Rose said.

Sharpie clacked her dentures and rolled over to the corner.

"Oh, Sharpie," Lark said. "Don't be such a grump!"

iPam zoomed over to her. They beeped and flashed at each other.

SHE DOES NOT LIKE YELLOW.

"Oh," Lark said. "Um, it's kind of too late now."

SHE IS JUST BEING GRUMPY, LOL.

"She's always being grumpy," Lark said.

iPam acted like a mother to the other robots. She broke up fights and scolded them when they got too rowdy. Or too grumpy, in Sharpie's case.

Clunk rolled on top of Chimney, who gave her a ride around the shed like he did every day. Data watched the world outside from her perch by the window.

"Hey, iPam, what's up with Data?" Penny Rose asked as she wiped a smudge of yellow paint off her hand with a rag. "She seems . . . different from the rest of you."

Penny Rose looked over at iPam, but her screen was blank.

"iPam?" Lark said.

DATA IS . . . SPECIAL. SHE SEES THINGS.

"What kinds of things?" asked Lark.

FUTURE THINGS.

The girls stopped what they were doing and turned to stare at each other.

"Like *what*, iPam! Tell us!" Penny Rose said. Her voice sounded high and squeaky to her ears.

SHE KNEW YOU WOULD PAINT THE SHED YELLOW. BEFORE YOU DID, FYI BTW.

"Wow," Penny Rose said. Her heart beat quicker. What if Data could predict whether or not she'd get into the Secret Science Society?

"That's amazing!" Lark said. She jabbed her paintbrush back into the can and turned to face iPam. "Can she tell our future? What has she seen lately?"

"Does she know what grade I'll get on my math test?" Penny Rose asked.

"Yeah, and whether or not my mom will buy me the new pair of binoculars I asked for?" Lark asked.

iPam's screen went dark.

"iPam?" Lark asked. "What has she seen lately? Please, please tell us!"

NOTHING. LOL.

"Come on, iPam, what has she said to you?" Penny Rose asked.

"Can we ask her questions?" Lark asked. "Maybe she could help us win the lottery!"

"Yeah!" Penny Rose said. The two girls looked at each other with wide eyes, then turned to iPam.

TTYL.

She turned around and rolled into the Lava Lamp Forest.

"Come on, iPam, tell us something!" Lark said.

"Please?" Penny Rose asked.

iPam rolled into the wall and stayed there.

"OK, we get the message," Penny Rose said.

"If what she says is true, that's pretty cool," Lark said.

"Most definitely! But I doubt iPam will let us ask Data about stuff," Penny Rose said. "She's pretty protective."

"Oh, well," Lark said.

Penny Rose couldn't let it go that easily. She kept wondering if maybe Data could tell her about her future with the Secret Science Society.

"I think we should put the proclamation in a safe place, especially with all this paint around," Lark said. "Like taped inside of this box." She walked over to the box in the corner and tapped it with her foot.

"Sounds good," Penny Rose said.

She still wasn't sure about the proclamation. Maybe her robots should be shared with the world. And since they were really her creations, maybe it was her *duty* to share them with fellow scientists.

Chapter Eleven

The following Saturday, while Lark was at her cousin's birthday party, Penny Rose headed out to the shed by herself with her mom's cell phone. If the lighting was good and if she could get a decent shot, she would take a few pictures of roboTown. Why not? They were just pictures.

The robots beeped their greeting at her. Fraction gave her an extra-big wave. Clunk rammed into her shoe, backed up, and did it again.

"Oh, Clunk," she said. "You are so silly!"

Data stared out the window as usual.

"Data, do you see anything at all about my membership with the Secret Science Society?"

Data's eye stopped spinning.

iPam rolled up to Penny Rose.

SHE DOESN'T SEE ANYTHING. ROFL.

"Oh, OK, no big deal," Penny Rose said, shrugging. "She doesn't have to tell me if she doesn't want to."

She plugged in the Christmas lights and the Lava Lamp Forest.

"I'm just going to hang out with all of you for a little while by myself. I think I'll take a few pictures, too."

She pointed the phone at the window. Clunk had joined Data, and the two stood on the windowsill staring outside. It was a sweet picture. Poignant, even. She pointed and clicked. Fraction and Sharpie were taking turns on the tin-can elevator. She took pictures of them riding it. She went on to take pictures of roboTown from every possible angle until she finally managed to get a shot with all the robots in it.

"Perfect!" She looked at the picture again and smiled. "See you guys later!"

When she got back to her room, she took the note from the Secret Science Society out of her desk and read it again. It was clear they just wanted a picture. She wouldn't be showing them the actual robots.

Lark's proclamation said nothing about pictures.

Penny Rose swiped through the shots. The one that showed all of roboTown with all the robots was the best by far. She zoomed in on it. The light coming in through the window bounced off the shiny metal of the robots, making them sparkle. The lava lamps and the Christmas lights glowed. Looking at the picture, it occurred to her that not only was it a cool science experiment—it was also a work of art. And architecture, come to think of it. Someone should see it other than just her and Lark. People should be given the chance to appreciate it.

Her heart thumped as she typed in: "THESE ARE MY ROBOTS AND THIS IS ROBOTOWN. SINCERELY, PENNY ROSE." She punched in the number and pressed send.

She exhaled.

"So that's done."

She shook her head. It was silly to get so excited. They probably sent the same note to fifty kids. Or it was a joke. She deleted the text and the pictures so her mom wouldn't see them. She was being a world-class doofus.

Her stomach grumbled. As she was walking down to the kitchen, her mom called to Penny Rose from her office.

"Dad's at his ukulele lesson. He made some kind of tuna fish before he left. It's in the fridge."

"OK," Penny Rose called back.

After checking out the tuna fish, which had leftover lima beans and quinoa in it, she decided to make an ordinary peanut butter and jelly sandwich. She poured herself a glass of apple cider and sat down at the kitchen table.

While she ate, she thought about the Halloween costumes she and Lark were making. Yesterday they had found two huge boxes and a can of silver spray paint in Lark's basement. Now all they had to do was find things to stick on the boxes to make them look like robots, like dials and bolts. After lunch she was going to poke around in the shed for just the right things.

She rinsed off her plate and her cup and put them in the dishwasher. Upstairs she could hear her mother's sad country songs playing. She always played sad country songs when she paid the bills. She said the songs matched her mood.

Thunk, thunk, thunk.

Penny Rose turned off the water and listened. It sounded like someone walking up the front steps and onto the porch. Probably just Dad coming home from his ukulele lesson.

The doorbell rang. It certainly wasn't Dad. Someone ringing the doorbell in the middle of the day on a Sunday afternoon in October was pretty obviously a stranger.

It couldn't possibly be the Secret Science Society. She had only just sent the text fifteen minutes ago. It took them weeks to look over her answer about the pencil.

And yet if she had been the one seeing a picture of her robots for the first time, she would want to see the real thing right away.

Penny Rose stood frozen in the kitchen. She wasn't sure she was ready to see who was on the other side of the door.

Chapter Twelve

"Penny Rose, can you get that, please?" Mom called.

"'Kay," Penny Rose answered, barely above a whisper. Her legs felt heavy, like she was walking through wet cement. She peered out the window.

Lily Proom was standing on the porch with her arms crossed. She was wearing her purple-fringed boots, the ones Penny Rose stared at longingly every day. Today they matched the purple sparkly scarf around her neck. Everything about Lily was cooler than other kids.

What on earth was Lily doing standing on her doorstep? If a giraffe wearing a beret had been standing there, it would have made more sense.

Lily rang the doorbell again.

Penny Rose slowly opened the door. "Hi," she whispered.

"I saw your text. We all did. Those robots are *really* cool. Go get them, and I'll take you to our clubhouse."

Penny Rose stood there for a moment, taking in Lily and her purple-fringed boots. Her heart was pounding so loud, she was afraid that Lily might hear it.

"You're a . . . member?" Penny Rose asked.

Lily laughed. "Yep!"

"Oh," Penny Rose said. Of all the kids in school, she had not expected the popular and pretty Lily Proom, who had always ignored her, to be a Secret Science Society member.

"Well?" Lily asked. "You coming?"

"I, um, my m-m-mom . . . I, well, really, I should, because if I don't, then . . ." Penny Rose stopped stammering and took a gulp of air. "I've gotta tell Mom, I think. I guess."

"Of course," Lily said. "But hurry, OK? Our meeting is beginning soon."

Penny Rose started up the stairs just as her mother came out of her office.

"Hi, I'm going to, um, a friend's house for a little while," Penny Rose said quickly. Lily had come in and was standing behind her. Penny Rose could smell her grape lip gloss.

Mom leaned over the banister. "Hello!" she said to Lily. "What's your name?"

Lily plastered a huge smile on her face. "I'm Lily Proom!"

"Oh, I know your mother!" She smiled back at Lily. "Love your boots!"

"Thanks!" Lily said. "We won't be long."

Mom waved her hand. "Don't worry. Have fun, you two!"

Penny Rose gulped. She wasn't sure that *fun* was the right word. Her palms felt sweaty. She wished she had studied her Conversation Starters harder.

Lily turned to her as soon as they were alone on the front porch.

"Grab your robots and let's go."

"Really?" Penny Rose said. "Um, I kind of—"

"We have to see them. We need to know they're real and not Photoshopped or something."

"OK," Penny Rose said. "They're in back."

Penny Rose jogged around her house to the back-yard. She opened the door to the shed and saw iPam rolling down the slide. Her gaze swept over the rest of the robots. Should she take all of them or just a few? It was a hard decision to make on such short notice. But if she took them all and something happened, she'd never forgive herself.

She spied Sharpie lurking in the Lava Lamp Forest. "You'll do," she said as she picked up the grumpy robot.

Sharpie gnashed her teeth together.

"Don't do anything unless I push your ON switch," she said. Her voice was stern but nervous. "Can you do that? It's really important."

Sharpie stopped gnashing her teeth and made a beeping noise, which meant she was talking to iPam.

iPam rolled over to Penny Rose.

SUP?

"Nothing. I just want to take Sharpie on a little walk, that's all." Penny Rose gave her a shaky grin and looked around the shed. Data stood on the window-sill as usual. Maybe Data could see Penny Rose's future with the Secret Science Society if she came with them.

"You, too," she said, picking up Data. "Come with me. It'll be fun."

She found her tool belt in the cardboard box in the corner. She buckled it tightly and slipped the two robots into the pockets. "Now remember, no movement unless I push the ON button! And even then, *do very little.* You have to pretend that you're not real."

She still wasn't completely sure this was a good idea.

She jogged back to Lily.

"Here they are," she said. She pointed to the two robots sticking out of the tool belt.

"That's all?" Lily said. Her brows drew together, forming a deep V above her long, straight nose. "Your picture showed a lot more than that."

"Um, the others got paint on them, and uh, they're all gunked up. So. Yeah. Paint."

Penny Rose looked down at the ground, hoping the excuse was good enough.

"OK," Lily said. "Let's go."

Penny Rose had a hard time keeping up with Lily, whose legs were approximately twice as long as Penny Rose's. When they got to the edge of Darkling Forest, Lily stopped.

"Stand still, I'm going to put this blindfold on you," she said, taking off her purple sparkly scarf.

"Blindfold?" squeaked Penny Rose. She could feel her pulse thumping in her neck. "Ummm—"

"We're still not sure if you're right for our group, and we can't have you knowing where our clubhouse is."

Goose bumps spread across Penny Rose's skin as Lily tied the scarf firmly around her eyes.

"How will I know where to walk?" Penny Rose asked. Her voice shook. She worried she might cry. This did not feel right at all.

She felt Data move slightly in the tool belt. Penny Rose squeezed her eyes shut and willed the small robot to stop moving. Data stopped. It was comforting, in a way, to know she was there.

"Don't worry. I'll lead the way," Lily said. She held Penny Rose's hand and tugged her forward, causing Penny Rose to stumble.

"Sorry," Lily said. "Oh, watch out for this branch." Lily stopped walking and held her hand tighter as Penny Rose stepped cautiously over the branch. "OK, you're good," she said once Penny Rose had cleared it.

Penny Rose could hear the scampering of wild creatures and the murmur of a distant brook as she and Lily walked farther and farther into the woods. It had rained the night before, and the mud made strange sucking sounds as they walked. When they came to the bottom of a small hill, Penny Rose smelled wet leaves and felt them slip under her sneakers and stick to her ankles.

She had never ventured very deeply into Darkling Forest. She and Mom had hiked one or two trails when they first moved to Skillington Avenue, but then Penny Rose had gotten busy with the robots. She would stare at it sometimes, wondering about all the treasures that it surely held. But the way it sat at the end of her block like a crouched animal was not particularly inviting.

Lily stopped walking. She dropped Penny Rose's hand.

"You can take the scarf off now," she said.

Penny Rose hesitated before pushing the scarf up to the top of her head.

"Wow," she whispered.

"I know," Lily said, nodding.

The structure before her wasn't a tree house, exactly. Tree houses were usually perched on tree branches, and this was on the ground. But it was definitely tree-like, with four huge maples acting as pillars on each corner.

Patchwork walls made of wood and scrap metal had been built between the trees. A perfectly square window hovered above the small door.

Penny Rose stood a few feet back while Lily strode up to it. She knocked three times fast.

"It's me," Lily said into the shut door. "I brought her."

Someone unlocked the door and pushed it open. Penny Rose squinted. She couldn't see who was there. Lily motioned for her to follow.

Penny Rose took a deep breath before stepping inside.

Chapter Thirteen

It took Penny Rose's eyes a moment to adjust to the darkness.

Jeremy Boils scowled at her from a beach chair opposite the door. His wild red hair looked like it hadn't been brushed in days.

Penny Rose tried to make her lips move, but they refused.

Jeremy Boils — scowling, angry Jeremy Boils — was part of the Secret Science Society.

"Are you going to come all the way in or what?" Jeremy asked.

Lily frowned. "Be nice."

Jeremy rolled his eyes.

Penny Rose wasn't sure she wanted to go in farther after seeing Jeremy roll his eyes, but her curiosity won out and she took two more small steps. She looked around while Lily settled into one of the beach chairs next to Jeremy's. Above their heads was a hand-lettered sign on a piece of plywood that said: THE LAB. Behind them were shelves jammed with books, beakers, microscopes, telescopes, Erector sets, and jars filled with items she couldn't quite make out in the murky light. There was a small table off to the side with stools situated around it that was not unlike the table she and Lark worked on in the shed. Paper cups, bottles, and some kind of big blobby thing sat in the middle of the table.

But what fascinated Penny Rose the most were the dozens of pictures taped to the wall. Faded school pictures of kids with braces and strange glasses. And there was writing. Penny Rose inched her way closer and saw that lots of kids had scrawled names and dates on the walls using all kinds of pens. Some, she saw, dated back to the 1960s.

"Did you bring the robots?" Jeremy asked. His deep voice made him sound much older than Penny Rose, even though he was just in the fifth grade.

"Um, yeah," she said.

"Well, come on, let's see them," Jeremy said. He leaned toward her in his seat.

She didn't like the hungry look in his eyes. She paused.

Someone knocked on the door.

"It's me!"

Lily unlocked the door.

Merry Zwack gasped for breath in the doorway. She wore a T-shirt five times too big for her, as usual. She smiled at Penny Rose, showing off the bright blue rubber bands on her braces.

Penny Rose wanted to pinch herself. *The* Merry Zwack just smiled at her! Popular kids had never smiled at her before. And apparently Merry was part of the Secret Science Society, too!

Penny Rose felt fizzy all over, like ginger ale was coursing through her veins. She smiled at Merry.

"I rode my bike as fast as I could," Merry said. "Did I miss anything?"

"Nope," Lily said. "We just got here."

"Good!" Merry said. She smoothed her hair and cleared her throat. "OK, so I'm Merry Zwack, and I'm the president of the Secret Science Society. My science specialty is the environment. I made a video on global warming and the things kids can do to help. It went viral."

She looked intently at Penny Rose, waiting for her response.

"I saw it. It was great."

The whole school had been talking about that video. It was even on the news.

Merry nodded and smiled, but somehow not in a braggy way. Penny Rose wished she had that kind of confidence.

"Jeremy is our engineer," Merry said. "He, um, also makes robots."

"I just made a Robotonator," Jeremy said. "The advanced version. They sell it at the Science Store. Where did you get your robot kit?"

Penny Rose swallowed. "I didn't make them from a kit. I made them from regular things, like cell phones and pencil sharpeners."

"Huh," Jeremy said. He squinted at her, as if he wasn't quite sure about something.

"And Lily is our entomologist," Merry said.

"I made my own beehive in my backyard," Lily said. "And last year I got an award for my ant farm."

"My dad's an entomologist," Penny Rose blurted out. She immediately worried that she sounded like she was boasting.

"Wow, that's so cool!" said Lily.

"Yeah!" Merry said. "My dad's just a boring old accountant."

Both girls smiled at her. Jeremy shrugged. "It's cool, I guess," he said.

Merry continued, using a very official voice. "So the Secret Science Society was started in 1969 by Betsy Bueller. You know about her, right?"

Penny Rose nodded. She was a fifth-grader who had gotten the whole school district started on recycling way back in the sixties. There was a framed newspaper article all about her hanging in the trophy case at school. She was a legend.

"Betsy wanted to have a place where kids could talk about science as much as they wanted to without feeling like weirdos."

Penny Rose knew that feeling well. Even Lark didn't seem very interested in talking about science. She saved her super-science discussions to have with her parents.

"We are also always striving to invent things that might someday help others," Merry said.

"Like the gym locker security system I'm working on," Jeremy said.

"And I sell the honey that my bees make at the farmers' market," Lily said. "All the proceeds go to Save the Bees."

"But we have to be sure that you are as science-minded as we are," Merry said. "We take our club really seriously. It's been around a long time. We heard about how you won the science competition last year in your old school, and we think you might be just right."

"How did you hear about that?" Penny Rose asked.

"We have ways," Jeremy said. He waggled his eyebrows at her.

Merry sighed in exasperation and looked up at the ceiling. "I saw the article about you while I was at my grandmother's house. I thought you'd make a great member, but you lived too far away. Then when I heard you moved here—"

"But you're not a member yet," Jeremy said.

Penny Rose wasn't sure what to say. She looked down at her feet.

"You don't have to rub it in, Jeremy," Merry said.

"Anyway," Lily said, changing the subject, "this week we're making a volcano using baking soda. I added the purple food coloring." She pointed to the big blobby thing in the middle of the table, which had long drips of purple down the side of it.

"Next month we're going to start working on our drone," Merry added. "But we're not sure yet what it will do." She shot a sharp look at Jeremy.

"It should spy on people," he said. "That's what drones are for."

Lily shook her head. "No, it should drop milkweed seeds over fields so that milkweeds grow, which will save the monarchs. Don't you think so, Penny Rose?"

Penny Rose paused. "I think both ideas are . . . interesting," she said. Taking a side against Jeremy did not seem like a good idea.

"See?" Jeremy asked.

"She's just being nice," Merry said.

"Whatever," Jeremy said. "Let's see these so-called robots of yours." He made air quotes around the word *robots*.

Penny Rose frowned. Her robots were real. They did not deserve air quotes.

Penny Rose squeezed Sharpie extra tight before pulling her out of the tool belt and setting her down on the floor.

"Ooooh! She looks amazing!" said Merry.

"Is that it?" asked Jeremy.

Penny Rose flipped the small robot's ON switch. The light at the top of her head flashed. Her teeth gnashed together. She rolled forward for a few inches, then stopped.

"Oh, my gosh! She's great!" Merry said.

"That's, like, the coolest thing I've ever seen," Lily said.

Jeremy didn't say a word.

"I have another," Penny Rose said. "Actually, I have five of them altogether, but I only brought two."

She set Data down on the wooden floor and turned her on. Data's marble eye rolled around. Her motor hummed. She slowly waved an antennae arm at them.

"I can't believe how amazing these are!" Merry said. "Did you make them all by yourself?" she asked, tilting her head to one side.

"I made them," Penny Rose said. She shifted from one foot to the other. "But—"

She looked at all of their faces. Lily raised her eyebrows. Merry smiled. Jeremy scowled.

"But what?" Lily asked.

"I had help with roboTown," Penny Rose said quickly. "That robot metropolis in the picture I showed you."

"I figured," Jeremy said. He crossed his arms and smirked.

"*Your mom* helped you with your metrics project," Merry said to him. "Remember?"

Jeremy shrugged.

"Who helped you?" Merry asked.

"Do you know Lark Hinkle?" Penny Rose asked. She knew that they did. Everyone knew Lark. She was the class weirdo.

"Oh," Lily said.

"She's weird," Jeremy said.

"Sorry, but we don't really have room in here for another member," Merry said.

And that was that. Lark was dismissed as quickly as recess on Friday.

Merry picked up Sharpie and ran her finger over Sharpie's dentures. "Where did you get these weird teeth?"

All at once Lily and Merry started shooting questions at her about how she made her robots. Penny Rose found herself talking to them almost the same way she did with Lark. In some ways, she found they were easier to talk to. They mostly understood the science, for one thing. She didn't have to explain too much about how she fit the batteries in or how she worked on getting the robots' arms to move. They nodded as she talked about her new idea for a solar-powered light for the shed and about the mug-warming invention that she had been thinking about. Even Jeremy seemed interested in that.

Before she knew it, she was in her own beach chair laughing about Mr. Moyes, the science teacher, and how his stomach always poked out of the bottom of his shirts.

At one point she glanced over at Data, whose marble eye spun ever so slowly. Did she see a future for Penny Rose and the Secret Science Society? Penny Rose couldn't wait to find out.

Chapter Fourteen

The sunlight in the Lab dimmed. Lily stood and removed the purple scarf from around her neck.

"It's getting late," Lily said.

"Yeah, I should get going," Penny Rose said.

"We'll be in touch," Merry said, smiling at Penny Rose.

Penny Rose wanted to ask if she had passed the test. She even practiced saying it in her head. *So did I pass the test?* It seemed like an easy thing to say, but for some reason the words stayed in her head.

The walk home was quiet. Lily slipped the blindfold off as soon as they got out of the forest.

"Those *are* really cool robots," Lily said when they got to Penny Rose's front porch. "See you at school."

"See you," Penny Rose said. She stood on the porch and watched as Lily started walking away.

"Um, Lily?"

Lily turned around. "Yeah?"

It was just the two of them, which was safer. Penny Rose gulped. "Do you think, um, that I'm, you know, I don't know, was I . . ."

"I'm ninety-nine percent sure you're in," Lily said. A small smile slipped across her face. "We'll let you know. Bye."

Penny Rose had to force herself not to jump up and down.

"OK, then. Bye."

Once she was inside, Penny Rose raced up the stairs, heaved open her bedroom door, and flung herself on her bed next to a startled Arvid.

"I did it!" she cried to the four walls. "At least I think I did! I'm in!"

She gazed up at the ceiling. The previous owner had painted a sky on it, with clouds and birds and a large swirling sun. She smiled as she stared at it. Arvid snuggled in next to her and curled himself up into a tight ball. She stroked him behind the ears.

Something poked her in her side.

Sharpie!

"Oops," she said. She sat up and took Sharpie and Data out of her tool belt. "You both were great," she said to them. "Thanks for doing what I asked. I'm sorry if it was weird."

She put them on her nightstand. Sharpie clicked her teeth. Data waved. Arvid hissed.

"Arvid, stop," she said.

Penny Rose heard footsteps in the hall. She quickly stashed the robots under her pillow.

Mom poked her head in the doorway.

"Did you have fun with Lily today?"

"Yeah." Penny Rose nodded thoughtfully. She hadn't thought it was going to be fun at all, and yet it turned out being lots of fun.

Mom smiled. "I'm going to help your father with dinner, or else we'll all die of starvation." She shook her head. "He wanted to make an applesauce and mashed potato casserole for dinner."

"You'd better hurry up and get down there," Penny Rose said.

Mom laughed. "Oh, I almost forgot. Lark called. I told her to call back after dinner. OK?"

"Sure," Penny Rose said, her voice cracking a little.

Her stomach clenched when she thought about talking to Lark. She couldn't tell her about the meeting with the Secret Science Society. That was probably a surefire way for a person to end her membership with a secret society. And what if she wanted to join? Then she'd have to tell Lark what Jeremy had said about her. It wasn't nice, and Lark wouldn't like it. Why tell her when it will only hurt her feelings? That was not the kind of thing a best friend does.

Or was it?

Penny Rose thought about Lark all through dinner. She wished Lark would just . . . what? Disappear? Understand? Both?

The phone rang while Penny Rose was rinsing off her plate in the sink.

"Can you get that, Penny Rose?" Dad asked.

"I'm doing the dishes," she said.

"It's probably Lark," Mom said. "You can do the dishes after you talk to her."

"But I want to do them now," Penny Rose said. She kept her back to her parents as she rinsed out her glass. "Otherwise they get all crusty."

"Well, someone needs to get it," Dad said, shoving himself away from the table. "I guess that someone is me!"

Just as he was about to answer, the phone stopped ringing. Dad shook his head and sat back down at the table.

"Honey, why didn't you pick up?" Mom asked.

"I told you, I want to do the dishes," Penny Rose said. "Besides, she'll leave a message."

Penny Rose still had her back to them and couldn't see their expressions. She didn't need to. She knew that they were both most likely giving her the Concerned Stare.

But something had changed. She felt different about Lark now — Lark's loud, scratchy voice; her huge sunglasses; her obsession with birds. She thought about how the Secret Science Society dismissed Lark right away, and how she hadn't stopped them.

She knew she was embarrassed. But she couldn't tell if she was embarrassed by Lark or embarrassed by herself.

Chapter Fifteen

The next day was Sunday. Lark called again in the morning while Penny Rose was brushing her teeth.

"Tell her I'll call back," she yelled to her mom.

After breakfast, Penny Rose took Sharpie and Data out to the shed. Chimney was waiting by the door as usual.

"Chimney, we're going to have to make a doggy door for you, except it will be a squirrel door."

Chimney scampered in and basked in the robots' warm greetings. Penny Rose placed Data in her usual spot by the window with Sharpie next to her. She squatted down on the floor and started rolling pennies with iPam.

"Hey, Data," she asked, "I really need to know something. Like, a 'future' something." She looked at iPam for the answer.

WHAT DO YOU WANT TO KNOW?

"Am I going to get into the Secret Science Society?"
iPam turned to Data, whose eye spun crazily.

GET A LOCK.

Penny Rose stopped rolling the penny to iPam. She
frowned at Data. "What does that mean?"

SHE MEANS FOR THE DOOR. TO THE SHED.

"Are you sure she doesn't mean that I should make
a squirrel door? Like the ones they have for dogs?
'Cause I was just thinking—"

iPam interrupted her.

SHE MEANS A LOCK. FOR THE DOOR.

"But that's not what I asked!" Penny Rose said.
Sometimes it was frustrating using iPam for every
single conversation. It made things ten times more
difficult.

SHE UNDERSTANDS YOUR QUESTION, FYI.

"iPam, can you just—"

Before Penny Rose could finish her sentence, Lark
barged in wearing her usual getup of sunglasses and
binoculars.

"You wouldn't believe what the birds left for
me today! It was the teeniest, tiniest green button
you've ever seen, and it was right in the middle of the

birdbath." She pushed her sunglasses up and sat down. "What were you talking to the robots about?"

"Me?"

Lark snorted. "Yes, you! I just heard you talking to them!"

"Oh, I was, um, gosh, I don't even remember."

Penny Rose got up and started digging through the box in the corner. "Hey, what do you think of a robot made of this?" she asked, holding up an electric can opener.

"It's fine, I guess," Lark said. She glared at Penny Rose in an unnerving way.

"Why do you keep looking at me like that?" Penny Rose asked.

"I called you last night, and you never called me back. In fact, I called you twice. And once this morning!" She folded her arms across her chest. "I figured I should just come over here, and now I hear you talking to the robots, and you won't tell me what you said. What's going on?"

"Nothing is going on," Penny Rose said. She put the can opener back in the box and rummaged around until she came upon a tiny toy train. "Do you think the robots would like this?" she asked, holding it up.

"You are being so weird."

"I am not!"

"Yeah you are!"

"You're the one who is always so weird!" Penny Rose blurted out. "Every single day of your life!"

It took a while for Lark to say anything.

"You think I'm . . . weird?" she asked in a shaky voice.

"You don't even try to be normal," Penny Rose said. "What with your weird gifts from the birds and everything."

No one moved, not even Chimney.

Lark stood. "Some best friend you are!" She glared at Penny Rose, then stomped over to the door.

"Bye," she said, yanking open the door.

"Bye," Penny Rose said. She tried pretending that she was just saying an ordinary goodbye on an ordinary day, but this, she knew, was not ordinary. She knew something big had just happened between her and Lark. And she wasn't sure if she was upset about it.

"She can be so strange," she said to iPam.

iPam did not text a word. Instead, she rolled over to the Lava Lamp Forest and stood facing the wall.

"Fine, be that way," Penny Rose said. She got up to leave. "Lark would hate the Secret Science Society. It's for her own good that I keep this a secret."

She peered over at iPam, who quietly stood by a blue lava lamp.

"Come on, Chimney," she said. "Time to go."

The squirrel followed her out the door. She closed it harder than usual.

"Everyone is so annoying!" she said to Chimney.

He blinked at her and scurried away.

Penny Rose spent the rest of the day in her room writing Conversation Starters. She wanted to be prepared just in case she bumped into any of the Secret Science Society members in the hallway at school.

But that night, before she went to bed, she found herself writing odd Conversation Starters, like:

1.) What is the best way to apologize to your best friend?
2.) Do you sometimes act like a jerk to your best friend?
3.) Does Lark hate me now? Do the robots?

"Arvid, I hope you still like me," she said before turning off her light.

Arvid closed his golden eyes and sighed.

Chapter Sixteen

When Penny Rose saw Jeremy at the bus stop the next day, she wasn't sure how to act. She glanced his way, but he stared straight ahead. She wondered if this meant they had decided not to invite her into the Secret Science Society.

She hadn't gotten in. She was sure of it. She stared intently at her sneakers as she waited to climb the steps of the bus.

Lark wasn't at the bus stop. This was not unusual. She was often late. When the bus pulled up, Penny Rose looked toward Lark's house and saw her slamming the door. Her hair was a tangled mess and her sunglasses were askew, making her look weirder than usual.

Penny Rose climbed onto the bus and sat in the front seat, where she and Lark usually sat. She slid her math textbook out of her backpack. After a few other kids got on, Lark raced up the steps, out of breath. Penny Rose looked up cautiously from her textbook.

"Hey," she said softly.

Lark passed her seat without saying a word.

Penny Rose's cheeks flushed. Lark had believed her about the robots when they first came alive. She could have made fun of Penny Rose or told her she was crazy and weird, but she didn't. She had acted just like a best friend was supposed to act, and now Penny Rose had messed it all up.

Penny Rose took out her pencil and a piece of paper from her backpack and wrote:

I'm sorry. XO PR

She folded it up into a tiny square, turned, tossed it to the middle seat where Lark was sitting, then turned around again quickly.

When Lily and Merry got on at the next stop, Penny Rose's heart sped up. She sneaked a peek at them. Merry gave her a quick smile as she headed to the back of the bus.

Lily brushed up against Penny Rose's jacket. "Sorry, Penny Rose!" she said.

"It's OK," Penny Rose said with a big smile. But Lily had already moved on.

Penny Rose snapped her head back down. She stared at her math textbook, but everything on the page might as well have been in Latin. Her ears, though, like Arvid's, were picking up the slightest sounds.

She jumped when she heard Merry squeal from the back of the bus.

"Ooooh! Can you BELIEVE it?" Merry said.

"No!" Lily said. "I really can't!"

Penny Rose didn't dare turn, but her stomach did a dance with each giggle they made. They were laughing at her; she just knew it.

Penny Rose peeked over her shoulder at Lark, who had straightened her sunglasses and was staring out the window. She was ignoring Penny Rose's note.

It was already an awful day, and Penny Rose hadn't even gotten to school yet.

When the bus let them out, Penny Rose walked as quickly as she could to class all by herself. She watched the clock all day and worried about lunch. She and Lark always sat with Laticia and Britta. Lark did most of the talking. Without Lark at lunch, Penny Rose would have to talk. She had not memorized the appropriate Conversation Starters for this situation.

When the bell finally rang, she took her lunch box out of her cubby and dragged herself down the hall to the lunchroom. It was going to be a long half hour. She looked for Lark but couldn't see her.

Just then someone grabbed her by the elbow.

Merry Zwack.

"Come with me," she whispered.

Penny Rose glanced nervously up and down the hallway as she followed her. They stopped at the library.

"Hi, Ms. Codell! We're just working on a project," Merry said.

Ms. Codell looked up from her computer and gave them a distracted wave.

Merry led Penny Rose to the farthest stack of the library, in the science section. Lily and Jeremy were sitting cross-legged on the floor eating their sandwiches.

Merry plunked down next to Jeremy and opened up her lunch box. "This is one of our meeting places," she told Penny Rose. "You'll know we're meeting here if this book is placed upside down on the shelf." She picked up a book with an old stain on the cover shaped like a protozoa. "It's a book about Madame Curie and it came out in 1969, the year the Secret Science Society started. If there's a meeting, we'll stick a note on page forty-four with the time and date." She shook her head. "No one ever takes this book out. Too bad. It's actually pretty good."

Penny Rose nodded and sat down on the floor next to them. She felt funny about eating in the library. It seemed wrong—like dancing in the grocery store or playing catch in the dentist's office. Some things just weren't done.

But no one seemed to mind, so Penny Rose took out the peanut butter and grape sandwich her father had made for her. She took a big bite. A grape shot out from the bread and landed on the floor.

Penny Rose froze. She looked to see who had noticed. They all had. She picked up the grape and put it in her lunch box.

"Was that a grape in your sandwich?" Jeremy asked. He wrinkled his nose. "Gross!"

Before Penny Rose had a chance to answer, Merry said, "I think it's cool! Like grape jelly only better! Very creative!"

She beamed at Penny Rose.

"So, before we make you a new member, we need to see the rest of your robots," Jeremy said. "You haven't passed. The Secret Science Society is a club for only the best scientists. We can't let just anyone in."

"Oh," Penny Rose said. She looked down at her sandwich but didn't take a bite.

Merry swatted her arm. "Don't worry about it!"

Penny Rose gave her a weak smile.

"We're meeting today after school," Lily said. "I'll come by to pick you up at three forty-five."

"Don't forget to bring the rest of the robots," Jeremy added. He had eaten his entire sandwich already, except for the crusts. He popped a stick of bright green gum into his mouth. Penny Rose could smell its minty freshness from her spot two feet away.

The others chatted about a YouTube video that showed the bubbling surface of Mars, but Penny Rose stayed quiet. She felt strange carting all the robots through the woods and allowing them to be handled by the Secret Science Society. And she felt even stranger doing all this after school, since that was the time she and Lark usually hung out in the shed. They had almost finished making their robot costumes.

But now that Lark wasn't speaking to her, maybe they wouldn't even go trick-or-treating together.

Even though Penny Rose had started the fight, and she felt bad about it, she wasn't sure she wanted it to end. She needed it to last a little bit longer. Like, until the others had seen the robots and officially let her into the Secret Science Society.

Chapter Seventeen

As soon as she got home, Penny Rose raced up to her room, found an old shoe box, and then ran out to the shed. Chimney was waiting for her patiently. Lark was nowhere in sight.

The robots rolled over to Penny Rose and Chimney as soon as they came in.

"Has Lark been here, iPam?" she asked.

NO.

"Oh," Penny Rose said. "I guess she's busy."

Penny Rose squatted down on the floor. "I need to take all of you somewhere today, OK? But you have to promise that you'll only move when I turn you on, and that you won't do anything fancy, like text me or anything. Got it?"

Penny Rose had forgotten that the robots talked among themselves. "Yes, I am. To the Secret Science Society's Lab. It's really cool there. You'll love it."

iPam's screen was blank.

"iPam? Is that OK?"

She paused.

I SUPPOSE. LOL.

"Great! I'm just going to put you in this box."

As long as the robots didn't act like they were alive, she saw no reason why she couldn't show them to the Secret Science Society. She was pretty sure that wasn't going against the proclamation. And they were her robots after all, not Lark's. She had created them. Lark only helped make roboTown.

Penny Rose carefully placed iPam, Fraction, and Clunk in the shoe box. She shooed Chimney out of the shed.

"Sorry, Chimney, but they'll be back soon."

She raced back to the house and waited in the front hall. Seconds later Lily hopped up her front steps.

Penny Rose opened the door and greeted her with a nervous smile.

"I'm going to Lily's house," she called to her father, who was working in his office with the door closed.

"'Kay," he called back. "Have fun!"

"Ready?" Lily asked.

Penny Rose nodded. They chatted about their social studies quiz until they got to the edge of Darkling Forest. Lily took off her purple scarf and tied it around Penny Rose's eyes.

Penny Rose held the shoe box tightly under her arm as Lily led her to the Lab. Once there, she took the scarf off of Penny Rose and then rapped three times on the door.

"Let us in!"

Jeremy unlocked the door and watched Penny Rose as she entered. He locked it again once she and Lily were inside.

Penny Rose felt a shiver of fear. Something about the way he looked at the shoe box was unnerving. His scowl scared her, and for a split second she considered leaving. She imagined running through Darkling Forest with her shoe box, jumping over tree roots and rocks. It was as if a little person entered her head, just for a split second, and yelled, "Get out now!" But Penny Rose didn't know how to get home. And she

knew the little person, or whatever it was, was just nerves. It wasn't real. Jeremy was just a kid.

The Secret Science Society *was* very real. She could smell Jeremy's gum and the mustiness of the Lab. The cool pictures on the wall, the science stuff on the shelves — it was all real. She felt as though she was just inches away from being part of it.

Someone knocked. Jeremy unlocked the door.

"Hi!" Merry said. Her big smile was aimed right at Penny Rose. "Hey, are the robots in there?" she asked, nodding at the shoe box.

Penny Rose nodded. "Except for the ones I already brought." She gripped the shoe box and stood completely still, like a soldier guarding a treasure.

Merry laughed. "Well, gosh, can we see them or what?"

Penny Rose started. "Oh, yeah, sure."

Merry walked over to the table and sat down on one of the stools. "Let's look at them here," she said, shoving aside the volcano.

Lily and Jeremy sat at the table. Penny Rose stood at the head and lifted the lid of the shoe box. All three Secret Science Society members seemed to be holding their breath.

Penny Rose took the robots out one at a time. First Clunk, then Fraction, then iPam. She stood them up in a row and turned each one on.

Clunk turned in a circle. Penny Rose knew she was nervous by how slowly and carefully she moved. A sparkle of sunlight hit her meat-thermometer head. Fraction waved one antennae arm and then stopped. She had stuck another heart sticker onto her calculator body. That almost made Penny Rose smile. The screen on iPam's belly flashed on and off.

"Whoa," Merry said. "Those are even cooler than the other two!"

"I like this one," Lily said. She reached over to pick iPam up.

"No, don't—" Penny Rose said before she could stop herself.

Lily looked at her and frowned, her hand hanging in the air near iPam. "Why not?"

"Oh, I guess, it's fine, I mean, I don't know," Penny Rose said. She shrugged. "They're a little fragile, that's all."

Before Penny Rose could stop him, Jeremy grabbed iPam.

"This is just an old phone," he said, turning iPam over in his hands. "The robots I make are all from specially designed parts. Not . . . junk."

Penny Rose's face flushed. She stared hard at him as he held iPam.

"She said they were fragile, doofus," Merry said. "Be careful!"

Jeremy didn't listen to her. He moved one of iPam's arms up and down. It came off in his hand.

"Oh!" Penny Rose said. Her heart beat faster. A lump formed in her throat as she watched Jeremy handle her robot. "Can you give her back to me, please?"

Jeremy was in his own world, though. He peered into the hole where iPam's arm was. "How did you attach it?"

Penny Rose couldn't answer. Her heart practically beat out of her chest.

"Give it back," Merry said sternly.

"I'm just looking at it," he said. He held iPam in the air, making her fly. "I'm a miniature Superman! Watch me knock over that other robot!" He swooshed iPam toward Fraction, who stood helplessly nearby. "Swishhhhh booooom!"

Penny Rose could feel the blood rushing to her face.

"Stop it!" she cried. "They're delicate!"

Jeremy didn't even look at her. But instead of smashing iPam into Fraction, he nudged her with his finger. Fraction tipped over backward.

"Jeremy! Why are you being like that?" Merry demanded.

Jeremy scowled at Merry. "They're not that delicate."

Penny Rose picked up Fraction and Clunk and put them back in the box. She looked over at Jeremy, who was still peering intently at iPam. He started spinning iPam's wheels between his fingers.

"Give it back to her," Merry said.

"It's more like a toy than a robot," he said. "Like something for a little kid. How cute." He made iPam dance on the table.

"Don't be a jerk, Jeremy," Lily said. "Give it back."

Jeremy swooshed iPam through the air again. Penny Rose couldn't even imagine what iPam was thinking.

"Jeremy, if you don't give her back that robot, I'm going to tell everyone at school that you're afraid of ghosts," Merry said quietly. She glared at him.

Jeremy stopped. He glanced over at Merry.

"That's right," Merry said. "Everyone."

Jeremy paused. He shrugged.

"Whatever," Jeremy said. He tossed iPam and her antennae arm into the shoe box.

"That was rude," Lily said.

"Totally," Merry said. "Just so you know, Penny Rose, Jeremy here is a world-class chicken. He's afraid of *ghosts*."

"I am not!" Jeremy said. "But the documentary I saw—"

"Oh, please," Merry said, shaking her head.

A rush of heat spread across Penny Rose's face. She could hear her blood coursing through her veins. Jeremy had tossed iPam. He had called her a toy.

She gritted her teeth and stood up straight.

"I have to go," Penny Rose said. She put the lid back on the box and blinked back tears.

This had been a big mistake.

Chapter Eighteen

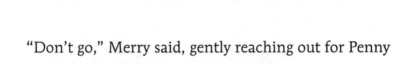

"Don't go," Merry said, gently reaching out for Penny Rose's sleeve. "He's just being Jeremy."

"Apologize to her, dork face," Lily said.

Jeremy turned away. "I'm sorry," he said. "I guess."

Penny Rose looked at each of them. Merry and Lily both gazed pleadingly at her. Jeremy glared down at the table.

Jeremy didn't seem like he wanted to be friends, but as she knew well, no friend was perfect. Lark wasn't perfect, and they had been good friends. Besides, Merry and Lily were nice, and they liked science as much as she did. Maybe she could get used to Jeremy.

"OK," Penny Rose said. "But I'm going to keep them in this box."

"That's fine," Lily said. "We just needed to see them in person."

"They are really cool!" Merry said. "I cannot believe how great they are! Did I tell you about that amazing robot I saw on the Discovery Channel? It walks and plays air guitar!"

"I saw that!" Penny Rose said. "That robot is the smallest robot in the world. It's in *The Guinness Book of World Records*."

"Someday I'd like one of my inventions to be in the Smithsonian," Merry said.

Penny Rose nodded. "That would be a dream come true."

Lily, Merry, and Penny Rose talked about other programs they had seen on the Discovery Channel. It was all three girls' favorite channel. Lark only cared about bird shows. She never wanted to talk about anything else, really.

While they talked, Jeremy rolled up little balls of foil from his gum and flicked them across the table. Mostly he stayed quiet.

Penny Rose looked out the window above the door. The sun was setting.

"Um, I, well, I should . . . can I . . . I mean, it's getting dark," she said. "I should probably go home."

Merry looked out the window. "Oh." She glanced over at Lily. "Can you take her back?"

"My stupid brother has all of his friends over right now. I want to stay here until they leave."

"I'll take her," Jeremy said.

Penny Rose's hands felt clammy all of a sudden. "I can find my own way back," she mumbled.

"In these woods? I doubt it!" Merry said. "OK, Jeremy, but be nice!"

"I will!" he said, frowning. "Jeez."

"Here," Lily said, handing him her scarf. "Bring it back to me tomorrow!"

Penny Rose looked at Merry. "Do we have to do that?"

"Sorry," Merry said. "We still need you to be blind-folded. We won't vote until Halloween. It's tradition."

"Oh," Penny Rose said. "OK." She smiled feebly. "Bye."

"Remember, Jeremy, be nice!" Merry said.

"Don't worry about it," Jeremy said. "I'll be nice."

Somehow Penny Rose doubted that.

Chapter Nineteen

Jeremy held Penny Rose tightly by the elbow as he rushed her through the woods.

Penny Rose stubbed her toe. Hard.

"Ouch." She hissed through her teeth.

"Oops," Jeremy said. "There's a branch there."

Penny Rose didn't say a word. She gritted her teeth until she heard the sounds of dogs barking and cars driving down her street. They were out of the woods.

"Can I take this off now?" she asked.

They walked for a few more moments.

"OK," he said finally.

Penny Rose lifted the scarf from her face. She saw the lights go on in her house at the end of the block. "I can go the rest of the way by myself."

Jeremy kept walking with her.

"So, do you just get your robot stuff from, what, junkyards?"

"Sort of," Penny Rose said. "I use things I find on the ground."

"I buy all my things from the Science Store. The owner there says he's never had a kid my age use such advanced materials. I doubt you'd be ready for that kind of stuff yet."

Penny kept quiet. She *liked* that her robots were made from repurposed materials. It made them unique.

"My house is just up here," she said.

"I know," he said.

He strode next to her, staring straight ahead.

"Where did you make them?" he asked.

Penny Rose didn't answer right away. That funny little person in her brain was shouting at her again. It was saying, *Don't tell him!*

"Oh, here and there," she said. They had passed Jeremy's house and were now standing in front of her house.

Jeremy looked over her shoulder into the backyard.

"What's that? A playhouse?"

"Something like that," Penny Rose said. Maybe if Jeremy thought the shed was a girlie thing, he wouldn't go snooping around. "It's got old dolls and stuff."

He continued to stare, craning his neck to look more closely.

"I've gotta go," Penny Rose said. She dashed up the steps of her front porch. "See ya."

"Yeah," he said, never taking his eyes off the shed. "See ya."

Once inside her house, Penny Rose's shoulders relaxed. Her house felt warm and inviting, with the goofy pictures of her as a baby hanging on the wall and the pillows with funny sayings, like REMEMBER, IF ANYONE ASKS, WE ARE A NICE, NORMAL FAMILY and RESERVED FOR THE CAT, on the worn red sofa. It all spelled home.

Arvid sauntered up to her and wound himself around her legs. She reached down to pet him, only to discover that her hands were still shaking.

"Good to see you, buddy," she whispered.

She could hear her parents in the kitchen singing along to some old rock song playing on their iPod. They were laughing at how bad they were.

She breathed a sigh of relief. It all felt so perfectly normal and ordinary. Even Dad's cooking smelled good wafting toward her.

She opened the lid to the shoe box. The robots were safe.

"Sorry!" she said. "I'll never let him pick you up again!"

WE DID NOT LIKE THAT.

"I know, I know! I'm so sorry! I'll fix you up good as new, I promise!"

"Penny Rose?" her mother called. "That you?"

"Yep!" she said. "I'll be there in a minute."

Penny Rose put the lid back on the shoe box, carried it up to her room, and put it under her bed.

"Just for now," she whispered.

She trotted down to the kitchen. Her mom was by the stove wearing a black and orange apron with a spiderweb design on it. Dad was staring at a cookbook on the counter.

"Hey there!" Mom said when Penny Rose walked into the kitchen. "I was starting to get worried. It's a little dark, honey."

"Sorry," Penny Rose said. She widened her eyes. "Are *you* cooking? For real?"

"I thought I'd give your father a night off," she said, winking at Penny Rose. "Besides, I miss cooking."

"Honey, are you set yet for your costume?" Dad asked. "Last I heard, you and Lark were going as robots."

Penny Rose sat down at the kitchen table. She picked up a saltshaker and started rolling it back and forth in her hands. "I was sort of thinking that I would stay home that night and hand out candy."

Dad peered up from the cookbook. Mom spun around. They looked at each other, then turned to Penny Rose and gave her the Concerned Stare.

Penny Rose had been thinking about this ever since her fight with Lark. Thinking it was one thing, though. Saying it out loud made it real.

Maybe even too real.

"Oh?" Mom asked. "Is anything wrong?"

"No," Penny Rose said. She continued to roll the saltshaker back and forth. "It's just that I'm a little old to be trick-or-treating."

Penny Rose was no such thing. But the thought of going out by herself—or, worse, with one of her parents—seemed pathetic.

Mom put on a bright smile. "Well, then, that means we'll all be together for Halloween instead of one of us here handing out candy. That will be fun!"

Dad shrugged. "If that's how you feel, Penny Rose, it's OK," he said. "But you and Lark had such big plans. Boxes and tubes and dials and silver spray paint and I don't know what else."

All those ideas seemed like ages ago now. They had never finished their robot costumes. Lark probably had a different costume made by now anyway. Even if Penny Rose started making her own robot costume today, it would never be ready in time.

After dinner she took the robots out from under her bed and put them on her desk.

"I'm so sorry," she said. She took a tissue and started wiping them off. "I can't believe that happened." iPam's screen lit up.

☹ ☹ ☹

"I don't blame you for being mad, iPam. I hope you can forgive me."

iPam's belly flashed, but she didn't text anything else.

"Fraction and Clunk, are you mad at me, too?"

The two robots spun in a slow circle so that they were facing away from her.

"First Lark, now you guys."

Penny Rose sighed. She gently put the robots back in the shoe box.

"I'm really, really sorry," she said as she put the lid back on and pushed it under her bed.

She wondered what Lark was doing right this minute. She felt a small pang in her heart, like the soft *plink* of a dime being dropped into a deep well.

Chapter Twenty

Penny Rose woke up Halloween morning feeling out of sorts. The wind howled. Creaky branches knocked together outside her window. Penny Rose hunkered down in her blankets. Arvid snuggled in close.

"Happy Halloween, Arvid," she said.

Arvid stretched and turned his back to her.

It didn't feel like a very happy Halloween. Mom had convinced Penny Rose to wear a witch hat while handing out candy, but even just thinking about doing that made Penny Rose sad. She and Lark had made fun plans. It was supposed to be the best Halloween ever. Now it all felt wrong.

Penny Rose pulled a sweatshirt over her pajamas and padded downstairs to the kitchen.

"Happy Halloween!" Mom said. She was eating oatmeal at the kitchen table.

Dad sat next to her reading the paper. When he pulled it away, Penny Rose gasped.

"Gotcha!" Dad said.

He had on a skeleton mask that was disturbingly real. He pulled it off and smiled at her. "Happy Halloween, sweetie!"

"Dad! You scared me!"

"I know!" he said. "Isn't it great?"

Mom flicked him with a dish towel. "Are you ever going to grow up?" she asked.

"Nope."

Every year her dad frightened her with some kind of Halloween prank. Last year he had put a fake spider in her cereal. Another year he pretended to chop off his finger. He had placed it on top of her pancakes. "Like a cherry," he had said.

Penny Rose plopped down in her chair. "Happy Halloween," she mumbled.

It was a Saturday, so Penny Rose had the whole day to mope. Right after breakfast, she went up to her room to get dressed. Then she hunted around for buttons and pennies. She stuck a bunch in her pockets and went out to the shed. She had apologized to the robots again and again after that trip to the Lab, but they were still mad at her.

The wind blew her hair every which way as she crossed the yard to the shed. Chimney stood near the door. Before going in, she peeked inside. Clunk spun in a slow circle while iPam rolled up and down a ramp. Data watched them from her perch. Fraction and Sharpie stood in the Lava Lamp Forest.

They seemed to move more slowly ever since her fight with Lark and their trip to Darkling Forest. She had given them new batteries, and yet they still moved and acted as though they were running low. She decided that after Halloween she would need to buy fresh batteries. Maybe the ones she had used were old.

But then there were the times when the robots ran without any batteries at all.

Penny Rose didn't want to think about that. All she knew was that something inside them was slowing them down. It might be fixed with a little tweaking from a screwdriver and a squirt or two of oil.

Penny Rose walked in timidly with Chimney at her side.

"Hi, robots."

The robots stopped.

"How are you?"

No one moved.

"Hello?" she said again, a little louder. "Are you guys still not talking to me?"

Penny Rose expected that at least Fraction would wave to her, but she didn't.

"I really am sorry," Penny Rose pleaded, a whine creeping into her voice. "I didn't know he would do that! Aren't you ever going to forgive me?"

iPam rolled over to her.

WHERE'S LARK. LOL.

"I told you," she said. Her cheeks grew warmer. She swallowed. "She's taking a little . . . break."

WHY.

"I don't know," Penny Rose said. She plunked down on a chair.

The robots stayed perfectly still.

"Anyway, it's Halloween. I thought you might like a little treat," she said. She dug the buttons and pennies out of her pocket. "You can make costumes with these like you did for your party."

No one budged.

"OK, I get the hint," she said. She got up to leave, then stopped just as she reached the door.

"I really hope you'll be able to forgive me."

She held the door open for Chimney, who scurried out.

"Bye, robots," she said. "See you tomorrow."

She shut the door gently. Before going back to her house, she decided to peek in the window again. The robots were back to their usual tricks. Clunk rolled from one end of the shed to the other. iPam slid down a ramp. Fraction and Sharpie stood in front of the mirror sticking buttons and pennies to themselves.

Data was at her usual perch by the window at the opposite end of the shed, marble eye spinning.

Penny Rose sighed. She didn't know what she would do if they never forgave her. It was awfully lonely without Lark or the robots.

That afternoon, while Penny Rose was in the kitchen putting candy in the dish shaped like a pumpkin, her father called out to her.

"Penny Rose, come here! This is interesting!"

She hurried into the family room, where her father and mother were watching a girl about her age being interviewed on TV.

"This girl reminds me of Lark! Listen!" Dad said.

Penny Rose settled down between them and watched as the girl pointed to things on a table.

"I got this one the other day," she told the interviewer. She held up a bright orange bottle cap. "And this I got the day before," she said, holding up a blue paper clip. "Every day the crows leave something for me. It's like . . . magic!"

"Oh, my gosh," Penny Rose murmured.

The interviewer looked into the camera. "Well, it's not quite magic," he said. "Crows have been known to give small items to people as a way of showing appreciation for being fed and taken care of."

"Honey, you should call Lark and tell her this is on!" Mom said.

"Mmmm," Penny Rose said. But she didn't move.

So Lark wasn't making it up after all. Crows brought gifts to people as part of their behavior.

It was actually *science.*

Chapter Twenty-One

When it was time to hand out candy, Penny Rose put on the witch hat. The brim was huge. She could pull it down over her face and hide if necessary.

Penny Rose brought the pumpkin dish to the front hall and pulled up a chair just inside the front door. Her parents had heard that their street got lots of trick-or-treaters, so they had extra candy in the kitchen. She had never handed out candy before. How much should she give away? Should she give two of the same kind or two different ones? It seemed like there should be candy rules for Halloween. It would make life a lot easier.

Mom came into the living room and put on some Halloween music. Dad put on his skeleton mask and started to dance to "Monster Mash."

"You'll scare the little kids!" Penny Rose said.

"With my dancing or my mask?"

"Both!" Penny Rose said.

Dad stopped dancing and took the mask off. He ran his fingers through his curly hair. "This thing makes my head sweat. I'm happy to keep it off." He walked over to Penny Rose and peered into the bowl on her lap. "Any Butterfinger bars?"

She dug through the bowl until she found one. "Not a lot." She held it out to him.

"Wouldn't be Halloween without Butterfingers!" he said.

He said this every year.

"Wait!" Mom said. She fiddled with her iPod until scary sounds came out of the tiny speaker. "I found this creepy sounds playlist. Listen to this!"

She played a wolf howling. Then bones rattling. A ghostly *wooooo* sounded especially spooky.

"Isn't it fun?" Mom asked.

"Yeah," Penny Rose said halfheartedly. "It's great."

When the first trick-or-treaters walked up the steps, Penny Rose hesitated. She looked up at her parents, who stood behind her.

"Give them two each," Mom whispered.

Penny Rose handed the firefighter and the fairy princess two tiny boxes of candy corn. They stared into their trick-or-treat bags as they scurried away.

Mom and Dad waved to the parents, who waited at the end of the walk. Soon there was a steady stream of ninjas, pumpkins, and skeletons. Penny Rose was glad that she didn't recognize anyone from school. Most of the kids were little.

At one point, while Penny Rose was doling out candy to a ballerina, she thought she saw Jeremy out of the corner of her eye, but when she looked again, it was someone in a wild white wig and a suit.

Just then, as two pirates clomped up the front porch, Penny Rose spotted something large and silver hurrying past her house.

"Honey, is that Lark?" Mom asked, squinting into the darkness.

It was Lark, and she was wearing a robot costume. Behind her was her mother, dressed up like a fancy witch. Her mom held a witch hat in one hand and Lark's little brother, Finn, with the other as she rushed to catch up with Lark.

"It is Lark!" Dad said. He broke into a huge grin. "Lark, come on over so we can see your costume!"

Lark stopped in her tracks. Her mom and her brother caught up to her.

"Honey, why are you going so fast?" her mom asked. Finn scowled. It looked like his mummy costume was squeezing him too tight.

Lark shrugged. "I don't know."

"Let's go see the Mooneys," Lark's mom said.

Penny Rose bit her lip. She peered at them from under the huge witch hat. Lark walked slowly up the path to their house. She wore one of the big boxes they'd found over black tights. She had painted the box silver and drawn a basic dial on the front. Her face was also painted silver.

Was Lark wearing the costume that they had planned together because she had forgiven Penny Rose? Or did she do it because it was the only costume she had?

"Hey," Lark said.

"Hey," Penny Rose said. She looked down into the pumpkin bowl and pulled out two Butterfingers. She handed them to Lark.

"I thought you two were going to—" Dad said.

"I love your costume," Mom said quickly. "You did a great job!"

"Thanks," Lark said. She turned to Penny Rose. "And thanks for the Butterfingers. They're my favorite."

"I thought so," Penny Rose said.

Lark stood on the porch for a moment, fumbling with her candy bag.

"Here's another Butterfinger," Penny Rose said. "For Finn."

"Thanks," Lark said.

Penny Rose was used to feeling awkward most of the time, but she wasn't used to feeling awkward with Lark. Conversation with Lark had always been so easy.

"It was nice to see you," Penny Rose said, feeling like a mom as she said it. "Good costume."

"Thanks."

Lark hesitated.

"I wanna go home," Finn whined. He tugged at one of the mummy bandages around his arm.

"Shhh, sweetie, just two more houses, and then we can go home and take your costume off," said Mrs. Hinkle.

"I'd better go," Lark said. She ran a few steps to her mother, then stopped and turned. She wiggled her fingers at Penny Rose. "Bye."

"Bye." Penny Rose's voice was just above a whisper.

She handed out candy for the rest of the night, and she could barely keep back her tears.

Eventually the street emptied out. Trick-or-treaters and their parents went home. The Secret Science Society, wherever they were, had probably come to a decision.

"I'm going up to bed," Dad said. He stretched and yawned.

"Me, too," Mom said. She headed toward the stairs. "Coming, Penny Rose?"

"In a minute," Penny Rose said. "I'm just going to make myself some cocoa."

Mom nodded. "It's an excellent night for cocoa." She blew a kiss to Penny Rose. "Nighty-night."

Penny Rose headed to the kitchen with Arvid at her heels. The tears that had been threatening to come out, the tears she had been fighting against all day and all night, streamed down her face.

Chapter Twenty-Two

Penny Rose took four deep breaths in the middle of the kitchen. She tore a paper towel off the roll and wiped the tears from her cheeks.

What if she was never really and truly friends with Lark again? Was the Secret Science Society even worth it?

She opened the cupboards and was looking for the cocoa powder when something out the window caught her eye. She stepped closer to it and stared outside.

In the corner of the backyard was the person in the white wig and suit. He was coming out of her shed.

Penny Rose ran to the back door and threw it open. The person in the wig stopped for a moment, looked at her, then dashed out the back gate.

Penny Rose darted out the door and chased after him. She caught a whiff of minty gum as she ran by the shed. *Jeremy!* Of course it was him. That strange getup was an Albert Einstein costume. She ran into the alley. He was fast and was already past the Gilmores' house next door. She ran after him, pumping her arms and forcing her legs to move faster than they ever had.

What was he doing in her shed? What if he had seen the robots move on their own? What if he took one of them?

Someone was bound to hear her if she yelled at him, so she just kept running. Her sneakered feet slapped the alley pavement. The air was cold in her lungs and against her face. It seemed like the closer she got to him, the faster he ran. He kept running until he got to Darkling Forest. Penny Rose could see the path that she and Lily took to the Lab. It had two huge elms on either side of it.

Jeremy looked back at her for a split second before he slipped into the darkness.

She knew he must be going to the Lab. But she had no idea how to get there.

She stood staring at Darkling Forest. It seemed darker and more ominous than usual. She had never

been to the Lab without wearing a blindfold. How would she ever find it?

She needed a plan, and she needed to think of one quickly. Unfortunately, she was not very good at thinking of plans quickly. All she really knew was that she had to find him. She ran back to her yard and through the back gate. The door to the shed was open.

Penny Rose held her breath as she approached. She stood just outside the doorway for what seemed like hours, afraid of what she might see if she went inside.

She finally gathered up her courage and crept into the dark shed. She groped for the Christmas lights and plugged them in.

Penny Rose gasped. It was chaos. Lava lamps lay on their sides. The ramps and the slide had been knocked over. Boxes were upended.

"Robots! Where are you?"

Penny Rose frantically dug through the mess that was once roboTown, picking through shoe boxes and toilet-paper rolls and train tracks.

Where were the robots?

Chapter Twenty-Three

"Robots, please! Where are you?"

Tears of frustration and anger streamed down Penny Rose's face. He stole the robots! *He stole the robots!*

She knelt in the middle of the shed and took another four deep breaths. She had to come up with a plan.

Then, from the corner of the room came a soft *meep.*

Penny Rose crawled on her hands and knees over to the corner where a big cardboard box sat and pulled it aside. There, huddled in the corner, were iPam and Sharpie.

"Oh, iPam! Sharpie! You're OK!"

She leaned over and ever so gently picked them up and put them in her lap.

"What happened?"

BAD BOY STOLE THE OTHERS. CHASED OUT BY CHIMNEY. WE HID.

"Oh, iPam, I'm so sorry! I'm going to find him, and I'm going to bring them all back! I promise!"

She picked up the two robots and stood.

"I'm taking you inside where no one can get you. And then—"

What?

She looked around her, thinking.

Lark.

Lark could help.

Lark *had* to help.

Penny Rose raced back into the house and tiptoed up the stairs to her bedroom.

Arvid greeted her with a yawn from her bed. She kissed each robot and put them both on her nightstand.

"Make sure they stay safe, Arvid," she told him.

iPam's belly lit up.

WE WANT TO COME.

173

"No, iPam, you can't. I can't lose you, too."

iPam spun quickly in a circle.

WE WANT TO COME WE WANT TO COME WE NEED TO COME WE NEED TO COME WE

"OK, OK," Penny Rose said. "But you're staying in my tool belt."

Penny Rose put on her tool belt, which already had a monkey wrench, scissors, wire, and a few nails in it. She found a flashlight in her desk and tucked it into the biggest pocket. She slid the two robots in carefully and gave them each a pat.

"Not sure what else I'll need," she said. "I guess I'll just have to figure it out as I go."

She pulled on a jacket and went out into the hall. Her parents' room was silent. They were probably fast asleep. She tiptoed to the top of the stairs and looked down.

Someone was standing next to the front door.

Penny Rose's heart pounded. Whoever, or *whatever*, it was had a pale, ghostly face and black holes for eyes.

Goose bumps spread across her skin. She was about to scream when she realized what she was seeing.

Her father had hung his skull mask on the hat rack by the door. She let out a breath.

Just then she had an idea. She walked toward it slowly. She jammed the mask into the pocket of her jacket and ran quietly into the kitchen. She grabbed the broom from the broom closet and put her mother's iPod and speakers into her tool belt.

Penny Rose scurried down Skillington until she got to Lark's house. She crept around to the back and saw that the light in Lark's ground-floor bedroom was on. Her window looked out onto the birdhouses, which were now all swaying in the breeze like tiny lifeboats bobbing in the sea.

Lark's shades were mostly pulled down, but Penny Rose could see through the space between the shade and the windowsill if she crouched. Lark sat at her desk, writing, probably her Nightly Bird Report. She was eating something.

Penny Rose tapped on the window. Lark started, saw Penny Rose, then frowned slightly and stood. She pulled the shade up, opened the window, and bent down so that her face was directly across from Penny Rose's. Lark's breath smelled like Butterfingers.

"What are you doing?" she whispered.

Penny Rose took a deep breath and let the words pour out. "I'm really, really sorry for what I said to you, which I know wasn't nice, and I've really missed you. But now I need your help because it has to do with the robots, and I know I can rely on you and that you always have great ideas."

Lark hesitated for a split second.

"Go on," she said.

Penny Rose told her the whole story. She told her about the note from the Secret Science Society and the secret meetings in the library and Jeremy's Albert Einstein costume and how Data had warned her to get a lock for the shed.

"So you told them about the robots?" Lark said. "Even after our proclamation?"

"They don't know they're alive," Penny Rose said. "But I'm scared that Jeremy might have seen them moving around in the shed. Now he's at the Lab in Darkling Forest, and I don't know how to get there!"

They stared at each other through the screen.

Penny Rose felt a small jab on her hip. "Oh, wait," she said. "Someone wants to say hi!"

She pulled iPam and Sharpie out of her tool belt.

"Oh, you guys," said Lark. "I've missed you so much!"

iPam's belly shone brightly.

LARK! IT IS U! LARK LARK LARK!

Sharpie clapped her metal arms together.

"They've really missed you," Penny Rose said. "Come on, can't you help us? For them?"

"OK," Lark said. "I'll help. But for them. Not for you, Penny Rose!"

Penny Rose nodded. "That's fair. I might have an idea, but I want to know what you think."

Lark listened to Penny Rose's plan. When Penny Rose was finished talking, Lark immediately pulled her desk chair over to her closet and climbed up on it. She reached her hand to the top shelf, grunting with effort, until she found what she was looking for. Penny Rose watched as she brought a cardboard box down from the shelf.

"I'll be out there in a second," she said. "Wait in the front yard."

Penny Rose crept around to the front of the house. She fidgeted with the mask in her pocket while she waited for Lark.

Time moved slowly. Penny Rose started to wonder what would happen if Lark never came out. It was possible she had decided not to help Penny Rose after all.

Just then she saw Lark heading toward her wearing a strange helmet with binoculars attached to it.

"What is that?" Penny Rose asked. "You look like an alien."

Lark handed another helmet to Penny Rose. "These are night-vision goggles. They'll help you see in the dark."

"Why do you—"

"Oma Maud gave them to me. They're for owling at night."

Penny Rose slipped the contraption over her head and looked at her feet. She could see the grass and the sidewalk more clearly. Everything around her—the trees, the leaves, the fences—glowed in shades of green, gray, and blue.

"These are cool!" Penny Rose said. "I can see so much better!"

"I know," Lark said, adjusting hers. "Now let's go."

They crept along the edges of the sidewalk by the streetlamps. Penny Rose had so much she wanted to

say to Lark, about how bad she felt and how much she missed her, but she wasn't sure how to say it without messing up.

"Why do you think he brought them to Darkling Forest?" Lark asked. "Why didn't he just bring them home?"

"I think because he saw me. He knows I don't know how to get to the Lab. He can hide them there."

"But why?"

"He probably wants to take them apart. To figure them out. If he saw the robots moving around, he would have to figure out why."

"But it's magic!" Lark said.

Penny Rose kept walking. She had never agreed with Lark about that, but this wasn't the time.

"So why don't we just barge in there and demand he give them back to us?" Lark asked.

"Because they keep the door locked anytime they're in there," Penny Rose said. "If I knock on the door, he's not going to just let me in."

"What if I knock on the door?" Lark said.

"Why would he let you in?" Penny Rose asked.

"I don't know," Lark said. "What if we just wait until he comes out?"

"Because the longer he's in there alone with the robots, the more damage he can do to them," Penny Rose said.

"You're right," Lark said. "I just hope he falls for it."

"Me, too," Penny Rose said quietly.

They walked until they reached the DEAD END sign at the top of Skillington Avenue. Darkling Forest loomed before them.

"We're here," Lark said, staring at the path that led into the forest. "Now what?"

"Um, this is the part I don't have planned," Penny Rose said. "I was kinda hoping you'd think of something. Like I said, I was always blindfolded. I don't know how to get there."

"That's just great," Lark said. "Because I have no ideas whatsoever."

Chapter Twenty-Four

They stood there at the edge of Darkling Forest, staring into its inky depths.

Finally Lark said, "Tell me what you heard after you put on the blindfold."

Penny Rose sighed. "Nothing, really. I don't know."

"Concentrate," Lark said. "When I'm listening for birds, I listen with my whole body — my ears and my nose and even my fingers. Does that make sense?"

Penny Rose shook her head. "Not really," she said. "But I'll try."

Penny Rose closed her eyes, and Lark held her arm. They took a few steps onto the path. She raised her chin up to the night sky as she listened. She could hear the wind. It grazed her face, cooling her skin. A tendril of hair brushed against her cheek. The same thing had happened when Lily first took her to the Lab. Small memories came flooding back to her. The smell of wet bark. The sucking sounds of her shoes in the mud. Crows cawing. A snap of a branch. A soft trickle of water.

Water. Nearby. She heard it now.

"I remember hearing that water," she said. She squeezed her eyes shut and concentrated with every muscle, tendon, and bone in her body. "And it was on my . . . right. Yeah. There's some kind of brook nearby."

"Great!" Lark said. "Let's keep walking! Was it always on your right?"

"I think so!" Penny Rose said. She could almost feel her ears heating up, straining to hear better.

"There's a fork in the path," Lark said. "Where should we go?"

Penny Rose bit her lip. "There was a place with lots of leaves," she said. "I remember feeling like we were walking through a leaf pile!"

"Great!" Lark said. "There's a pile of leaves to the left!"

They trudged through the slight dip in the path filled with leaves.

"There's a place where Lily said to watch my step," she said. "There was a branch."

"Good!" Lark said. "We're going to get there! I just know it!"

Lark helped her step over the branch. They walked a few more paces.

"There's another fork," Lark said. "Now what?"

Penny Rose squeezed her eyes shut tighter. She couldn't hear the brook. The wind had died. Darkling was silent.

Snap!

Penny Rose's eyes shot open. Lark looked as nervous as she was.

Snap! Whish!

Something was coming toward them. Leaves rustled as it moved along the path.

Penny Rose held her breath. Whatever it was, it was very, very close. And it did not sound human.

Neither girl spoke.

Snap!

It stood a few feet away. Penny Rose squinted, but even with the night-vision goggles, she could only make out a small dark shape.

The thing stood still. It rose onto its hind legs, exposing its white belly.

Penny Rose stared, mouth open.

"Chimney!" she said in a loud whisper. "It's you!"

Chimney bounded toward them, his black-smudged tail twitching with excitement.

"Oh, Chimney, am I glad to see you!" Lark said.

The robots started moving in Penny Rose's tool belt. She took them out and showed them to the squirrel. They clacked and buzzed and beeped with joy.

CHIMNEY!! HOW R U? WE HEART YOU!

"Chimney, if it hadn't been for you, all the robots would have been stolen!" Penny Rose said. "You chased Jeremy out before he could get all of them!"

Chimney kept standing on his haunches.

"Why is he just standing there?" Lark asked.

"I don't know," Penny Rose said.

"Wait!" Lark said. "I bet he knows where the Lab is!" Chimney twitched his tail and got onto all fours. He turned and started bounding off down the path on the right.

"Let's follow him!" Penny Rose said. She put the robots back in her tool belt and scurried after Chimney.

"We're following a squirrel through the woods at night on Halloween," Lark said behind her. "This is nuts."

Penny Rose nodded. "Most definitely."

Chapter Twenty-Five

They followed Chimney as he leaped nimbly over tree branches and stones. The forest grew darker the deeper they went.

"Is that it?" Lark asked, pointing.

Penny Rose looked up. It was the Lab all right. She could see the dim outline of the strange little hut. The lights were on. Someone was inside.

"That's it," Penny Rose said. "I bet he's there now."

"Maybe we should make it here," Lark said. "Then carry it with us. We'll have to be extra quiet as we walk, otherwise it'll spoil the whole thing."

Penny Rose nodded. She hoped this worked. She remembered Lily and Merry teasing Jeremy about being afraid of ghosts. If she could make something that looked creepy and ghostly enough, Jeremy *might* run out of the Lab and leave the robots behind.

In any case, it was the only plan they had.

She gathered leaves and stuffed them into the mask, but when she fitted the mask onto the top of the broom, the leaves kept falling out. Of course they would! Why hadn't she thought of that?

"Tie the bottom of it with string," Lark said.

"I don't have any," Penny Rose said.

iPam stirred in her tool belt. It felt like she was jabbing Penny Rose with one of her arms. She took iPam out.

THERE'S WIRE IN UR TOOL BELT.

"Oh!" Penny Rose said. "Why didn't I think of that?"

"Because you're not a super-cool robot," Lark said.

Penny Rose put iPam on the ground. She took Sharpie out of the belt and stood her next to iPam. Chimney let out a small squeak. He hopped over to the robots and bent his head down so that they could stroke his tufted ears.

"They're like a family," Lark said. "We've just got to find the others!"

Penny Rose dug the spool of wire out of her tool belt, cut a piece off with the scissors, and twisted it around the bottom of the mask. She held it up for the robots, Lark, and Chimney to see. It looked a bit like an unfinished scarecrow.

"He needs something," Lark said. She looked around on the ground.

"Like what?" Penny Rose asked.

"I dunno," Lark said, keeping her eyes on the ground. "Like arms, or something." She bent over and picked up a branch. "Here, tie this to it to make a cross."

Penny Rose cut another piece of wire off the spool and used it to fasten the branch onto the broom.

"Good," Lark said. "And now we do this." She unzipped her hoodie, slipped it onto the broom, and pulled the hood onto its head. Their scarecrow was now complete, except that it was a lot creepier than any scarecrow Penny Rose had ever seen.

"OK, you two, back in the belt," Penny Rose said to the robots.

The robots gave Chimney one last pat on the head. Penny Rose picked them up and carefully put them

in her tool belt. She took her mom's iPod and the two tiny speakers out of the belt and hooked them all together.

"Perfect!" Lark said. She picked up their fake ghost and glanced over at the Lab. "It's time to get going."

Penny Rose nodded. "I guess." She adjusted her night-vision goggles and hiked up her tool belt.

"Here we go," she whispered into the darkness.

Chapter Twenty-Six

As they came closer to the Lab, they heard someone talking. They crept along the narrow path until
they were only a foot away from the front door. They
crouched down on either side of it. The crack between
the door and the siding was big enough for Penny
Rose to peek through. She took off her night-vision
goggles so that she could look in.

Jeremy was on his cell phone. He was sitting at
the table and still wearing his Albert Einstein costume. Data, Clunk, and Fraction were in front of him.
Fraction was facedown on the table, and Clunk was
missing an arm. A lump formed in Penny Rose's throat.

"Mother, I've got everything I need, don't worry. Yes, of course it's fun. Sleepovers are fun. I'll be home before breakfast."

He paused. Penny Rose could hear the distant tinny sound of his mother's voice on the other end.

"It's only two blocks away! I can walk two blocks in broad daylight, Mother."

He paused again. His mother seemed to be going on and on about something.

"I have to go. I can't keep calling you every fifteen minutes. None of the other boys do. I'll be fine."

He clicked the phone off, sighed, and shook his head. After a moment or two of contemplation, he leaned in close so that his face was only inches away from Clunk.

"If you move, I will get you anything you want. Just do it again. I know you can. I saw you."

The robots didn't budge.

Jeremy stood. He paced around the small room, then stopped.

"I can take off another arm, you know," he said menacingly. "Would you move if I did that? Huh?"

His eyes glinted in the dim light of the Lab. He stood in front of the table with his hands on his hips.

"Well? Move, you dumb robots! Move or I'll make you into a toaster!"

Penny Rose shot a quick glance over at Lark. She could see that, like her, Lark had had enough. Now was the time.

Lark walked carefully over to the door with their handmade ghost. She raised it slowly above her, so that its head was in the center of the window above the small door.

Penny Rose tucked the speakers under her arms. She had cued up "Shrieking" from her mom's playlist. She pressed play. Nothing happened.

She looked over at Lark, who was holding the ghost facing into the Lab. Lark frowned.

"What's wrong?" she mouthed.

Penny Rose shrugged. She turned the iPod around in her hands until she finally saw what the problem was. She shook her head. The speakers weren't on! She slid the button on each of them to ON, put them on the ground, and pushed play again.

EEEEEEEeeeeeee! Eeeeee oooooo eeeeeee!

Penny Rose jumped. Her nerves were amped, but the shrieking was way louder than she'd expected.

"Who's there?" Jeremy cried. Penny Rose peered in

through the crack again. Jeremy was looking around the small room. "Where are you?"

Penny Rose dug her flashlight out of her tool belt, turned it on, and shone it up at the ghost.

Jeremy saw the flash of light and looked up at the window. His eyes bulged. A strangled gurgling sound came out of his mouth.

"Go away!" he said, backing up toward the wall. "Go away!"

Penny Rose pressed "Shrieking" again on the playlist. The eerie sound filled the woods.

Jeremy crouched. He glanced around the small hut wildly and ran toward the door.

Penny Rose turned off the flashlight. She waved both arms at Lark, who was standing in front of the door, but Lark didn't see her. She was too busy moving the ghost up and down in the window.

The doorknob jiggled. When it turned, Lark lurched out of the way, falling into the bushes. Penny Rose flattened herself against the side of the Lab.

Jeremy screamed and ran out the door.

"GO AWAY! LEAVE ME ALONE! MOMMMMMY!"

He ran out of the Lab holding his bowed head in his arms for protection.

He never looked up. He never looked back. He just ran and ran and ran with his arms wrapped around the Albert Einstein wig on his head until he was completely out of sight.

Chapter Twenty-Seven

Penny Rose helped Lark get out of the bushes. Once Lark was standing, Penny Rose picked leaves off of her sweater.

"It worked," Lark said.

"It did," Penny Rose said. "It really did."

"He's a fast runner," Lark said.

"And a loud screamer."

They looked at each other, then burst into laughter.

"MOMMMMY!" Lark said in a high, shrill voice. "Mommy, there's a ghost!"

"And his head is stuffed with leaves!" Penny Rose said.

"And he's wearing a Gap hoodie!" Lark said.

They doubled over. Lark fell to the ground, tears streaming down her face.

"I don't think he'll ever come back," Lark said, catching her breath.

"Not without his mommy!" Penny Rose said, which sent them both into fresh peals of laughter.

Penny Rose felt a jab in her side. She took iPam and Sharpie out of her tool belt and put them on the ground. Chimney emerged from the bushes and joined them.

"We did it!" she told them. "We did it, we did it, we did it!"

WHAT ABOUT CLUNK AND DATA AND FRACTION? FYI BTW, THAT'S WHY WE'RE HERE.

"You're right," Penny Rose said. She picked them up. "Let's get them home."

Chimney and Lark followed Penny Rose through the small door of the Lab. The salty lump formed in her throat once again when she saw Fraction face-down on the table.

"Oh, Fraction," she whispered, picking her up.

Data's marble eye started to spin. Clunk raised her one arm up in the air and beeped. Fraction didn't move.

Chimney clamored up the leg of the table. Penny Rose placed iPam and Sharpie on the table with the others. Robots and squirrel fell into a gleeful reunion of beeps, whirs, twitches, and spins. All except Fraction.

Everyone was completely still as Penny Rose turned her this way and that, trying to figure out what had happened. All her parts were there. She gave Fraction a gentle shake, but she didn't move.

"I don't understand," Penny Rose murmured. She pressed CLEAR on the small keyboard, then each number and symbol. Her screen was still blank. "Technically, she should at least be able to calculate, but I can't even get her to do that."

Lark stood next to her. "She's lost the magic," she whispered.

Penny Rose didn't want to agree with her, but deep down inside she worried that it was true. If it truly was magic, she had no idea how it worked. Science she could deal with. Magic was a complete mystery.

"Let's take them all back to the shed," Penny Rose said. "Maybe I can find something there that will fix her."

Lark put her hoodie back on while Penny Rose gathered up the robots, the fake ghost, and the iPod.

They wordlessly slipped their night-vision goggles on and headed toward the path.

The walk back through Darkling Forest was a quiet one. When Penny Rose heard the brook nearby, she knew they were close, but it didn't bring her any joy or relief. If Fraction — dear, loving Fraction — was gone forever, Penny Rose wasn't sure what she would do. How could she go on making robots knowing that someday they might die? It occurred to her that she had never really considered how *real* they were until just now.

Chapter Twenty-Eight

Lark's house was dark. Mrs. Hinkle hadn't noticed that Lark was gone. They kept walking until they got to the shed. Penny Rose took a deep breath before pushing open the door.

"What the—?" Lark began. She stopped in the doorway and gaped.

"Yeah, I forgot to tell you," Penny Rose said. "He made a huge mess while he was looking for them. iPam said Chimney chased him out. A lot of roboTown was wrecked."

"What a doofus," Lark said. "Or maybe he's a dweeb."

"He's definitely a dork," Penny Rose said.

They sat at their table. Chimney hopped onto the window ledge to watch. Penny Rose took out all of the robots and lined them up so that they could see everything. She stood Fraction directly in front of her.

"So," Lark said. "What now?"

Penny Rose sighed. "I could take her apart and put her back together again," she said. "Maybe."

"Maybe," Lark said. She fidgeted with the string on her hoodie.

"Or I could try new batteries? What do you think, iPam?" Penny Rose asked.

iPam motioned to the other robots. They conversed for a while in their odd little way. Data's marble eye spun faster than it had in days.

"Well?" Penny Rose asked.

MAKE IT LIKE BEFORE.

"What?" Penny Rose asked.

WHAT IT WAS LIKE WHEN YOU MADE US. MAKE IT LIKE THAT.

"Like a reenactment!" Lark said.

"Oh," Penny Rose said. She hunched over and put her head in her hands. "I don't remember!"

Lark stood. She paced back and forth. "OK, let's think this through. What time of year was it when you made Fraction?"

Penny Rose kept her head in her hands, thinking. "September. Definitely September. I remember talking to her on my birthday, and that's September nineteenth."

"Good!" Lark said.

Penny Rose raised her head. "Oh, gosh, but I had started them all before that," she said, frowning. "The thing is, I would make changes here and there. I didn't work on one robot until she was done. I worked on them all at once."

"OK, OK, good," Lark said, still pacing. "What time of day did you work on them mostly?"

"In the morning. Or at night. Or the afternoon."

Lark stopped pacing. "So basically anytime at all."

Penny Rose nodded.

"What else?" Lark asked. "Did you play music or have the same snack or anything?"

"No, nothing like that," Penny Rose said. She looked around the shed. So much had changed since then. It hadn't been yellow, for one thing. RoboTown wasn't there. She had been alone back then. All she had were the robots.

"Well," Penny Rose began. She wasn't sure she felt comfortable saying the next part, but she knew that for some reason it was important. "I was, you know, *alone* most of the time. You weren't . . . here."

Lark nodded slowly. "Oh, right. We weren't friends yet."

Penny Rose thought back to that time in her life, when it had been just her and the robots. She had spent so many hours talking to them. They were her friends. Her only friends.

"But I wanted a friend back then," Penny Rose said quietly. "I really, really wanted a friend. I —"

Penny Rose stood and abruptly turned away from Lark. She went over to the window and gazed into the night sky.

"What?" Lark asked.

"Before they were alive, I used to pretend the robots were my friends," Penny Rose said simply. "I did that a lot. I was always hoping for a real friend." She paused. "I guess I sort of . . . wished for a friend, in a way. Even though that is not very scientific. But then we met. And the robots. And even . . . the Secret Science

Society." Her cheeks flushed. She looked down. She had been so lonely back then.

She turned around. Lark nodded slowly. "That's it."

"It is?" Penny Rose asked.

"Yes," Lark said. "First we'll make everything like it was before. And then" — she paused and looked away — "you'll have to pretend that you have no friends at all."

Chapter Twenty-Nine

Penny Rose blinked.

"OK," she said. She remembered what it was like to have no friends. But she didn't really want to go back to that time.

"Let's make the shed like it was back then," Lark said. "We'll clear all this stuff out," she said, nodding her head toward the many boxes and toilet-paper rolls and lava lamps.

The girls got to work, quietly moving everything out of the shed. Most of it, they realized, would have to be redone anyway. The paper-clip chandelier had been crushed. The bubble-wrap wallpaper was torn. The slide lay in two pieces on the floor.

"What a mess," Penny Rose said.

Lark shrugged. "It'll be fun to put it back together again. Besides, I have some new ideas."

Penny Rose stopped. She turned to Lark.

Penny Rose didn't want to ask Lark about their friendship. She was too scared of the answer. But she didn't *not* want to ask it, either.

"Does that mean we're friends again?"

Lark paused. She bit her lip. "You were not a very good friend to me, Penny Rose."

"I know," Penny Rose said. "But I tried to apologize! I sent you a note on the bus! You never even said anything back."

"What note?" Lark asked.

"It was the day after I said that mean thing to you," Penny Rose said, flushing at the memory of her harsh words. "I folded up a note and threw it back to you. Remember?"

"I never got it."

Something lifted in Penny Rose. She felt lighter than she had in a long time. "Oh," she said quietly. "I thought maybe you never wanted to be my friend ever again."

"All I wanted was an apology," Lark said.

Penny Rose paused. "I'm so sorry, Lark," she said.

Lark gave her a quick nod. "Apology accepted."

They looked at each other and smiled.

"If it wasn't so late, I would go make us some raisin toast," Penny Rose said.

"We don't have time for that now," Lark said. "But tomorrow we will. Most definitely."

"Most definitely."

Once all of roboTown was moved out, the shed looked sad and small. Penny Rose stood in the middle of it and slowly turned around.

"It looks so weird this way now. So empty."

"Yeah," said Lark. She hovered in the doorway. "OK, I'm going to stand out here while you, I dunno, do whatever it is you did back then."

After Lark left, Penny Rose sat down at the table, where she had lined up all the robots. She picked up Fraction.

"Remember how it was before?" she asked Fraction. She held her in both hands. "I used to ask you how to get a friend." She slumped in her chair. "Maybe I should have asked you how to *be* a friend."

Penny Rose replaced Fraction's batteries. She tightened a screw in her back. She pushed her number buttons, then CLEAR.

It was no use. Nothing happened.

"I've been so dumb," Penny Rose said. "I had you guys and I had Lark. Then I had to go and mess it all up."

The robots, who had been watching quietly, all moved toward her. Clunk spun in a circle, as if trying to cheer her up. Data stroked her hand. Even Sharpie tried to comfort her by gently nibbling on her arm with the dentures.

iPam whirred to a stop inches in front of her.

WE STILL HEART YOU, FYI BTW.

"Thanks, iPam," Penny Rose said. A tear slipped down her cheek. "I'm sorry I was so awful. To you. To the other robots. To Lark. I was a doofus and a dweeb and a dork all smooshed in together."

The robots did not disagree with her.

"Fraction," she said, holding her in the palm of her hand, "if you're still in there, I hope you know how much we miss you and love you. You are a true-blue friend, and I'll never, ever forget that. I wish you would come back to us. I really, really do."

She held Fraction close to her heart. The shed was silent. She squeezed her eyes closed and wished with all her might.

"Please, please, please."

She put Fraction and the other robots on the floor and blew them a kiss.

"I guess it really was magic," she whispered. "And I guess I ruined it. I'm so sorry."

She opened the door, letting in a cool late autumn breeze. It swirled around her, lifting the pages of a notebook on the floor before whooshing out the door again.

Chimney twitched his tail, hopped off the table, and scampered through the door and into the night.

"Well?" Lark asked when she saw Penny Rose emerge from the shed.

"Nothing happened," Penny Rose said. "She didn't wake up." As hard as she tried to control it, Penny Rose's voice came out wet and wobbly.

Lark did what any good friend would do. She let Penny Rose cry without saying a word.

Chapter Thirty

Penny Rose picked at her caterpillar-shaped pancake. Her father had added frozen mango chunks to it that hadn't quite defrosted.

"The day after Halloween is always a little bit of a letdown," he said, wiping his hands on a dish towel.

Mom sat across from her, eating toast. "Would you like some toast, honey?" she asked. "Some nice *plain* toast?"

"No thanks," Penny Rose said. "I think I just ate too much candy last night."

The front door opened. Penny Rose could hear Lark's quick, light footsteps skipping down the hall. It was such a familiar sound, and it made her a little happier.

"Hi, everyone!" Lark said, breezing into the kitchen. "Happy Day of the Dead!" She disentangled her hair from a long green scarf and pushed her sunglasses on top of her head.

"Lark!" Mom said, beaming. "It's so good to see you!"

"Would you like some pancakes?" Dad asked.

"No thanks," she said, glancing at Penny Rose's plate. "I already had breakfast."

"Too bad," Dad said. "Mango pancakes are my specialty."

"Ready?" Lark asked. She had a fierce look in her eyes.

Penny Rose stood.

"Yep." She bit her lip. "We've got some stuff to do in the shed," she said.

"Sounds great!" Mom said.

Dad smiled. "Have fun!"

As soon as they stepped through the back door, Penny Rose stopped. "I don't know if I can do it," she whispered to Lark. "What if nothing has changed?"

"What if it *has* changed?" Lark asked. "You'll never know until you go in and see!"

Last night they had loaded everything back into the shed before leaving. They placed Fraction on the floor in a puddle of moonlight, which Lark was certain would help her somehow. It felt sad to be going back to such a broken place, especially not knowing whether Fraction was dead or alive.

When they were steps away from the shed, Chimney darted across their path. His tail was high and twitchy. He scurried back and forth in front of them.

"What is up with you?" Lark asked.

He ran around and around in small circles before pausing by the door to the shed.

"I guess he wants to go inside," Penny Rose said. She held the doorknob but didn't turn it.

"Come on," Lark said. She gently nudged Penny Rose's shoulder.

Penny Rose turned the doorknob and pushed open the door.

The robots, who were frozen in place, started moving when they saw who it was. Clunk zoomed up to them and did four quick spins. Sharpie clacked her dentures and waved. Data rolled her marble eye.

Penny Rose scanned the room for Fraction. She was still in the same spot on the floor. She sighed and looked at Lark, who shrugged.

"Good morning, everyone," Penny Rose said solemnly. "I hope you guys are happy to be together again."

She and Lark plopped down in their chairs. Penny Rose rested her chin on the table. Lark slumped.

"Well, you tried," Lark said.

"It wasn't enough," Penny Rose said. "I wish I knew what else to do."

The robots rolled toward them, clanking their arms together. Chimney made strange chirping sounds.

"What's up?" Lark asked them.

They whirred up to the two girls' feet and tapped rapidly on their sneakers. iPam's belly flashed on and off.

"iPam, what is going on?" Penny Rose asked.

iPam turned around to Fraction and beeped.

LOOK.

Both girls looked, but Fraction hadn't moved.

"Maybe they're sad," Lark said. "Maybe they want us to have some kind of service for Fraction."

"Like a funeral?" Penny Rose asked. "Is that what you want, iPam?"

NO NO NO NO NO NO NO NO

iPam started rolling toward Fraction.

"OK, OK," Penny Rose said. "Just tell us what you want."

When iPam was barely an inch away from Fraction, the unimaginable happened.

Fraction's arm moved.

It was a slight movement, but it was movement all the same.

"Did you see that?" Lark asked.

"YES!"

Penny Rose stood and stared as Fraction's other arm moved.

She was moving! Dear sweet Fraction was moving once again!

"You did it!" Lark said, high-fiving her. "You're a scientific genius!"

Penny Rose shook her head. "I don't think science had anything to do with this," she whispered.

She went over and crouched next to Fraction.

"How are you, my little friend?" she asked.

Fraction lifted both arms to her.

"Oh, Fraction! I'm so glad you're OK!" Penny Rose picked her up and held her close to her heart. "What would I have done without you!"

Penny Rose put Fraction down on the table. She whirred over to Lark, who gave her a kiss on the top of her calculator head. She moved slowly, but she was moving, and that was all that mattered. She was alive again!

Lark looked at Penny Rose. "This is so cool! She's back!" She clapped and stomped her feet. "Oh, and I almost forgot!" she went on. "The birds left me a few extra-special things this morning."

"Really?"

Lark nodded and reached into her pocket. She dug out two dimes and a piece of candy corn. "They also brought this," Lark said. She reached into her other pocket and took out a folded piece of notebook paper.

"When I saw this piece of paper this morning, I just *knew* everything would be OK!" she said. She unfolded the tiny square and taped it above the door.

In the middle of the square was a small red heart sticker.

"There. We'll always keep it where we can see it."

Chapter Thirty-One

Jeremy did not show up at the bus stop that Monday, which was fine with Penny Rose. She and Lark sat in the front seat, like they always did. Lark chatted about how Finn cried the entire day before about Halloween being over and how her mom had burned five pieces of toast that morning, which beat her record. Penny Rose hadn't realized how much she had missed Lark's constant chatter. She settled back into her seat and listened to her friend. She felt so light, like a cement block had been lifted from her shoulders.

Merry and Lily climbed onto the bus at the next stop. They smiled at Penny Rose and paused next to her seat.

"Hey, Penny Rose!" they said in unison.

"Hi," Penny Rose said softly.

"How are you doing?" Merry asked.

"Um, great," Penny Rose said.

Lily and Merry looked at each other and smiled.

"See you soon!" Lily said. She attempted a wink at Penny Rose. It looked more like a twitch.

Lily and Merry made their way to the back of the bus, giggling the whole way.

"What's that about?" Lark asked.

Penny Rose shrugged. "We're sort of friends now. I guess they're just being nice."

Before lunch Penny Rose found a note from the Secret Science Society tucked into her locker.

You have passed! You are now an official member of the Secret Science Society! Lily will pick you up today after school for our meeting. Wait for her in your front yard at 3:30.

Congratulations!

Sincerely,

The Secret Science Society

Penny Rose showed the note to Lark during recess.

"What are you going to do?" Lark asked.

"I'm not really sure yet," Penny Rose said, staring at the note. "But I'll think of something."

Lily and Merry were friendly to Penny Rose all day. It was nice to feel wanted, but it was a new feeling for Penny Rose, and she wasn't sure what to do with it. She had never been part of a group before, much less with the popular kids.

When she got home, she reread a few entries in her Conversation Starters notebook, but nothing really fit for this particular circumstance. She decided to wing it. Since Penny Rose had never really winged anything in her whole entire life, she felt quite bold.

Lily showed up at exactly 3:30 wearing her purple-fringed boots. She smiled at Penny Rose.

"Congrats!" she said.

"Thanks," Penny Rose said. She did not smile back.

"I'll show you how to get to the Lab," Lily said. "It's really pretty easy."

Lily strode down the path with her long legs. The fringe on her boots swayed as she walked. Birds sang to one another in the trees. Penny Rose couldn't help but notice that everything was much less scary in Darkling Forest during the day. She decided she should really spend more time there. Maybe Lark could teach her bird-watching.

When they got to the Lab, Lily knocked on the door and said, "It's me."

The lock clicked. Merry opened the door and smiled at Penny Rose. "Come on in!"

Penny Rose let out a small sigh of relief when she saw that Merry was the only one in the Lab. Merry sat at the table and motioned for Penny Rose and Lily to do the same.

Penny Rose cleared her throat. "Where's Jeremy?" she asked.

Merry frowned. "He quit," she said.

"Really?" asked Penny Rose.

"Yeah, he said we weren't science-y enough, or something like that. Who knows. He's weird."

"He sort of bugs me," Lily said. She smoothed the fringe on her boots with her fingers.

"Anyway!" Merry smiled at Penny Rose. "That is not what this meeting is about! This meeting is about *you*, Penny Rose! We want you to be our newest member! We think your robots are amazing!"

Lily smiled and nodded. "We especially like the one with the dentures—what's her name? Toothy?"

"Sharpie," Penny Rose said.

"Yeah, Sharpie! She's funny!" Lily said.

Merry leaned over and rifled through her backpack until she found a green folder and a purple marker. "So, in order to join, you'll have to sign an agreement," she said, suddenly acting very businesslike. "It says that you won't divulge any of the Secret Science Society's secrets." She took a piece of paper out of the folder and slid it and the purple marker across the table to Penny Rose. "Sign on the dotted line, please."

Penny Rose was afraid that her hands would tremble if she picked up the paper, so she looked down at it and kept her hands on her lap. After she read it, she looked up. Both girls stared at her with expectant grins.

"I can't sign this," Penny Rose said.

"Wait, what?" Merry asked, frowning.

"I can't sign it. It's wrong."

"Why?" Lily asked.

Penny Rose took a moment to gather her thoughts.

"Well, even though I did make all the robots, Lark helped me with roboTown. A lot. In fact, there wouldn't even be a roboTown if it wasn't for Lark."

"Yeah, but it's your robots we really love!" Merry said. "They are so cool!"

"I'm sorry," Penny Rose said, pushing her chair away from the table. "I can't do this without Lark. She's my partner. And" — she took a deep breath — "she's also my best friend. And best friends don't do that to each other."

Penny Rose stood. "If you want me, you'll have to take Lark, too." She started toward the door, then stopped. "She's really nice. And she knows a lot about birds, which is ornithology, which is a science."

And with that, Penny Rose walked through the door, closing it gently behind her.

On her way back to the shed, she could swear the birds in Darkling Forest sang louder than they ever had before.

Chapter Thirty-Two

Over the next few days, Penny Rose noticed Jeremy Boils acted differently around her. If they were on the same side of the street, he would cross it. If she was walking into school and he just happened to be walking in, too, he would stop until she went through the doors.

It was as if he associated that whole horrible night with her and her robots. As if she had somehow conjured up the ghost. Which she had, of course.

No one had ever been afraid of Penny Rose before. And if she was being completely honest with herself, she would have to admit she liked it.

"When I walked into the gym today, he stared at me so hard that he didn't even notice the basketball! It bonked him on the head!" Penny Rose said.

"That is crazy!" Lark said, laughing.

Penny Rose and Lark were sitting on the floor of the shed, making a new obstacle course while the robots hummed around them. iPam tried out the ramp. Clunk plugged and unplugged the Christmas lights. Sharpie sharpened a pencil. Even Data, who usually stood off to the side, seemed unusually happy as she rode Chimney around the shed.

Fraction stood right next to the girls, wearing the necklace Lark had made for her out of little beads shaped like pumpkins. Every so often she'd pat Lark's shoe or tug Penny Rose's shoelaces.

"I can't believe how well Fraction is moving around now," Penny Rose said.

"I know!" Lark said. She handed Fraction a dime, which she promptly balanced on her head.

Lark's expression changed. She frowned as she cut a toilet-paper tube in half. Penny Rose knew exactly what she was thinking about.

"Have you decided yet?" Penny Rose asked.

Lark shrugged. "No, not really."

"I understand," Penny Rose said. "I'm not sure what I would say, either. But I'm definitely not going to be a member without you, and that's that."

The day before, Lark had found an invitation tucked into her locker. It was from the newly formed Secret *Sisters* Science Society, and it was asking her if she'd like to join.

"It could be fun," Penny Rose said. "Merry and Lily are nice."

"They didn't want me before," Lark said. She looked down at the floor. Fraction immediately rolled over her shoe and gave her a friendly *beep-beep*. Lark smiled at her.

"How does she know when we're upset?" Lark asked, picking Fraction up and looking right into her face. "It's . . ."

"Magic," Penny Rose said.

Lark grinned. "Most definitely."

"You know, you didn't like me before you met me," Penny Rose said. "You thought I might be a doofus, a dweeb, or a dork."

"I know," Lark said.

"Anyway, you don't have to decide today," Penny Rose said. "It can wait."

The sun came out from behind a cloud and filled the shed with its late afternoon glow. It was warm for November. Penny Rose could hear a gentle wind in the trees. She opened a window to let it all in.

"Oh, I almost forgot!" Penny Rose said. She dug into her bag and took out a sign that she had made the night before. "I thought the old sign needed to be changed. There was one word that was way off."

She held up the new sign.

Don't Come in —
We're Creating

"Perfect," Lark said.

Penny Rose smiled. "Most definitely."

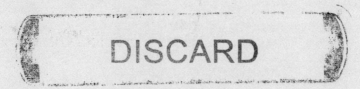